The Magic Dolphin

A Young Human's Guide to Beaches, Sea Level Rise
and Living with the Sea

Written and Illustrated by

Charles Pilkey

The Magic Dolphin

Cover Illustration by Charles O. Pilkey
Writing and Interior Illustrations by Charles O. Pilkey
Book Consultant: Orrin H. Pilkey

ISBN 978-0-9996903-0-7
1) beaches 2) sea level rise 3) marine science
4) environmental issues 5) juvenile fiction 6) science fiction
First printed in the United States

Printed by CreateSpace

For Kensho ... The future is yours.
Make it a good one ...

Contents

Foreword

Learning to live with the sea is critical, for our spiritual and physical well-being are closely linked to the health of the world's oceans. Food, medicine and more than half the oxygen we breathe come from the sea. Yet we continue to regard the ocean as a dumping ground for our wastes and as an underwater supermarket for our culinary needs. The sea is neither. It exists independently of humanity and the plants and animals that live in the sea and on beaches have as much right to life as we do.

Now a big collision is about to occur along the world's shorelines. On one side the pile-up involves the rising sea, which is causing beaches to retreat toward land. On the other side is the mad rush of people building houses on the same land that the rising ocean waters will soon claim. Something's got to give and it will be today's youth who will have to solve the problems caused by climate change.

As Maria and Arion travel the sea on the back of a magic dolphin, they have many adventures. Each adventure brings new knowledge and understanding. In Greenland they witness ice calving and learn how global warming causes sea level rise. In England they discover a broken castle, pounded over the centuries into ruins by the hungry waves, illustrating the perils of building too close to the sea. While exploring a ship-wreck on Namibia's Skeleton Coast they are nearly eaten by lions, but come to understand that the non-human life living on a beach doesn't mind sea level rise; as the shoreline re-treats, the beach life does the same. The kids learn a similar lesson on a barrier island off the coast of Colombia. There they watch fishermen move an entire village back from the receding shoreline. This gives Arion and Maria the germ of an idea for what must be done to save their own house from the inevitable advance of the sea.

The Magic Dolphin was written in the gloom of a world much diminished from the world of the previous generation. Global warming, pollution, overfishing and the relentless extinction of species have made our world less bright, less colorful, less diverse. But these trends are not inevitable and with some effort can be reversed. If we instill in kids a sense of wonder at the miracle of the sea and a scientific understanding of how the sea (and beaches) work, then perhaps they will become wiser stewards of the planet than we have been. They will do what we have failed to do — heal a damaged biosphere and keep the magic of this world alive.

Orrin Pilkey, 2017

Acknowledgements

We are happy to acknowledge the support of our friends Eva and Olaf Guerrand Hermes and their Santa Aguila Foundation. These two dedicated people are good friends of beaches. They worry about marine pollution, the problems caused by coastal erosion, the mining of beach sand and the damage that seawalls do to beaches. Underlying their concerns is an awareness that sea level rise is going to create many problems for beaches around the world. For all these reasons, Eva and Olaf started the world's foremost coastal/beach website: **coastalcare.org** (run by the ever-cheerful Claire Le Guern Lytle). We urge the readers of this book to visit the coastal care website to learn more about how beaches work and what we must do to pre-serve them for future generations. It will make reading *The Magic Dolphin* all the more meaningful and interesting.

Also, special thanks to Wallace Kaufman for his input into writing children's books, to Tonya Clayton for her help with editing and to Norma Longo, who proofed and edited several versions of the book.

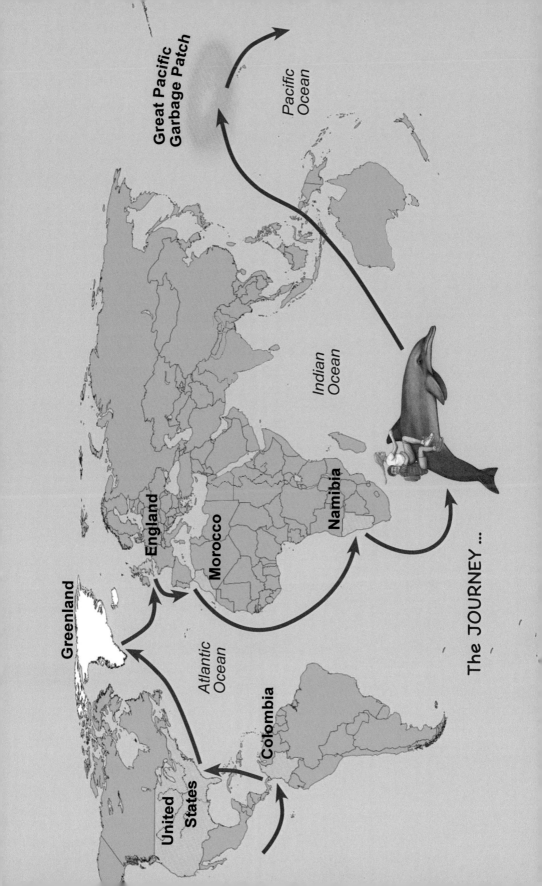

Great Pacific
Garbage Patch

Pacific
Ocean

Indian
Ocean

England

Morocco

Namibia

Greenland

Atlantic
Ocean

Colombia

United
States

The JOURNEY ...

The Magic Dolphin

A Young Human's Guide to Beaches, Sea Level Rise
and Living with the Sea

Written and Illustrated by

Charles Pilkey

1 Make a Wish

n the blackest night I've ever known the wind roared and great claps of thunder shook our little beach house so hard I felt my bed tremble. Through my bedroom window I watched rain streaming sideways, as if someone had turned on a giant garden hose. Waves marched their way up the beach, one after another, pounding the sand with fierce intent. I waited in the dark, wondering if the angry surf would spill over the dunes and drag our house out to sea.

Sometime after midnight the wind began to calm and I fell into a troubled sleep. But at the first hint of dawn, I got my sister Maria up. After a hurried breakfast, we left a note on the kitchen table for our parents, explaining where we'd be. Then we grabbed some plastic bags and rushed down to the water to look for the shells we knew the storm had washed in. And that was how we found the Magic Dolphin.

We were surprised to see our neighbor standing on a dune in his pajamas, drinking coffee and talking excitedly on his cell phone. His house was closer to the water than ours. Sometime during the night the sea had washed away his deck, scattering pieces of wood and broken furniture across the sand. We had been lucky … this time.

It was a perfect morning for beachcombing. Except for a lone surfer, the beach was deserted. The storm had dragged from the deep all sorts of marvelous creatures — squishy jellyfish, red and purple sea fans and creepy horseshoe crabs that crawled through the sand like spiky-tailed dinosaurs.

Maria even found a Scotch bonnet, a rare and beautiful shell.

"A gift from the sea," she called it.

Further down the beach we passed the house damaged by last year's hurricane. It was leaning awkwardly down the face of a dune with its windows still boarded. But the storm must have taken away the "Do Not Enter" sign that was there the day before.

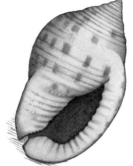

Scotch bonnet

I looked at Maria. She said nothing but I knew what she was thinking. *Would the same thing happen to our house someday?*

We lived on one of the many barrier islands that line the coast of the Carolinas, some of them miles long, others less than a mile. Ours was one of the smaller islands. Every year fierce Atlantic storms battered our little island home and seemed to push the sea ever closer to our house. Mom and Dad were already talking about selling the house and moving back to the mainland. It was something I hated to think about. We all loved the beach and I couldn't imagine living anywhere else.

The sun was just peeping over the horizon when Maria announced we'd reached the end of the island. It was time to head back. No houses stood on this part of the island, only dunes and a cluster of dead cedars bent nearly double by the wind and bleached bone-white by salt and sun. The trees poked through the sand like broken fingers. Beyond the trees, I could see the old lighthouse rising from the sea between our island and the next island.

I stopped to examine my bag of shells. The motion spooked a ghost crab, which scooted sideways and disappeared down a hole.

"My bag's nearly full and I still haven't found a single shark's tooth," I complained.

Fossil shark's teeth are as common on Carolina beaches as fleas on a dog. So far the day had been a complete letdown.

"Maybe you'll have better luck on the way back."

"Hope so," I said.

All things old and dirty fascinated me. And the older and dirtier a thing was, the greater was its hold on my imagination. On my bookshelf, crammed between science and mythology books, were trilobites, snakeskins,

Ghost crabs live on many of the world's beaches. They usually scavenge for food at night.

arrowheads, a cat skull and even a small dinosaur bone I'd found out west. Most of my friends dreamed of becoming football players or rap stars. I always knew I'd be a geologist.

"Let's rest awhile before we head back," suggested Maria.

"Good idea," I said, yawning mightily. Neither of us had slept well last night, what with all the thunder and wind.

We stretched out on the beach and spread our shells on the sand. I had more unbroken shells but Maria had found some rare ones, including the Scotch bonnet and an angelwing.

I closed my eyes and listened to the sound of waves. The sun was a warm caress on my eyelids. From far away the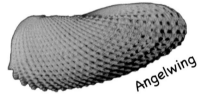

Angelwing

laughter of gulls lazed across the water. The world became a gentle lullaby of wind and wave and gull sound.

I must have dozed off. When I opened my eyes Maria was standing a few feet away studying the lighthouse.

"Look at that old lighthouse, Arion," she said. "It's right in the middle of the water."

I stood and brushed sand from my clothes. We'd seen the lighthouse many times before, of course, but never from this close. Waves left over from the storm were breaking on its foundation, sending spray high into the air.

"And it seems to be leaning into the sea," Maria continued.

I couldn't tell if the lighthouse was leaning. But Maria was right. It was in the middle of the water, a long way from land.

"I wonder how it got there," she said.

"The storm made the tide unusually high," I offered, knowing from experience that storms usually bring higher than normal tides.

"It's possible," she answered. "Or it could have been the moon. Very high tides happen on a full moon and last night the moon was full."

Maria loved everything about the moon. In her room was a giant poster of the Apollo moon landing. And on her ceiling and walls she stuck little plastic moon shapes that glowed in the dark.

"Maybe they built the lighthouse on land but the land sank," I theorized. "You know, like Atlantis."

The Morris Island Lighthouse

"Maybe," said Maria. "It's a pretty cool looking building, don't you think?"

"Yeah, I guess."

My sister had always been a little weird. She liked to dress up and pretend she was a grownup. I guess all girls are that way. But Maria also spent her free time reading books about old houses and bridges and stuff. I knew for a fact she'd already checked out every book in the public library on architecture, ancient or modern. She even read the books with no pictures! On her desk were wooden models of famous buildings like the Taj Mahal and the Empire State Building. If I didn't do something quick we'd waste the whole morning staring at a bunch of wet bricks.

What was needed, I decided, was a distraction. Luckily, at that moment I spotted a pile of driftwood at the water's edge next to the salt marsh.

"Must be some good shells over there," I said, pointing to the driftwood.

That got her attention. But as we approached the pile we soon realized it wasn't driftwood at all. It was something else. And it was stirring.

"It's a dolphin!" exclaimed Maria. "And it's alive!"

The dolphin was bigger than any dolphin I'd ever seen, much bigger than the ones at SeaWorld. The storm must have washed it ashore. The poor animal was hopelessly tangled in a fish net, struggling to get back into the water. But it was weak and could barely move. A small, wrinkled eye looked right at me. On top of its head an air hole opened and something like a long sigh came out.

"Come on, Arion. Help me push it back to the sea."

We pushed with all our strength but couldn't move the poor creature. Not even a millimeter.

"We could go for help," I suggested.

Maria looked around. No one was in sight. "The tide is still going out. By the time we get help, the dolphin might die."

"What should we do?" I asked.

Then the dolphin spoke.

"Free me," it said in a small, creaking voice that was little more than a whisper.

Maria looked at me. Her eyes were wide. Her face had gone white as milk.

"Did you hear ...?"

"It talked," I said simply.

I was not surprised to hear a dolphin talk. I'd always figured animals were cleverer than people realized. And dolphins were especially smart. Why shouldn't they talk?

"Free me," pleaded the dolphin in a rasping, high-pitched voice. "I'll grant you any wish. Cut the net and set me free!"

Taking the sharpest shells we could find, we tried slicing the net. But the strands were too strong. Then I remembered that I was carrying my pocketknife. Our task became much easier. The more I cut, the more the dolphin was able to move. First it moved its head. Then it wiggled its flippers and its tail.

Finally, it pulled itself free of the net. With great effort, by twisting its body from side to side, the animal slid into the sea, trailing clouds of sand as it slipped into deeper water.

The dolphin was so happy to be swimming again it jumped and danced across the surface of the sea, even turning back flips over the waves. For several minutes it frolicked back and forth, until it glided to the water's edge where we were standing.

"Greetings, little friends. My name is Delphis and I'm a magic dolphin. Because of your kindness, I will grant you one wish. Can take you places and show you wonderments you've never dreamed of."

Maria didn't know what to say so she introduced herself.

"My name is Maria and this is my little brother Arion. Uh ... nice to meet you."

"Hi there," I said. *Do dolphins shake flippers or rub noses when they meet?* I wondered.

"Did you say you would grant us a wish?" Maria asked.

"That's how it usually works. You rescue me. I take you places," said the dolphin.

I was curious. "Like what kind of places?" I asked.

"Anywhere you care to visit. Long as it's over water. As you may have noticed I'm not much good on land."

Now it's not every day that one meets a magic dolphin, especially one willing to grant you a wish. So we took some time to consider the possibilities.

"Maybe he can take us to Spanish treasure ships with gold and jewels and old cannons," I suggested.

"It might be fun visiting old shipwrecks."

"Or better yet. Let's go see the *Titanic*."

"My teacher said it's cold and dark at the bottom of the sea. We should go someplace warm, like a coral reef."

"Coral reefs have sharks, don't they? I'm scared to death of sharks. Disney World would be a lot safer."

"Disney World's not near the sea, silly."

"Maybe we could go to another beach and look for shark's teeth."

"And shells," said Maria. "That's a great idea!"

Turning to the dolphin, she said, "Can you take us to another beach where we can go shell hunting?"

"Shore thing," said the dolphin.

"But we have to be back before lunch," added Maria.

"Why shoretainly."

"And Mom will be totally irritated if my shoes get wet."

"No worries. Just clamber on my back, keep your shoes high and we'll be off."

We left our shells on the beach (except the Scotch bonnet, which Maria refused to part with) and climbed onto the dolphin. I was surprised at how smooth and slippery its back felt, something like wet rubber. Maria wrapped her arms around the fin. I held onto her waist as the dolphin backed away from the shore and made for deeper water.

Faster and faster he went until, to our astonishment, the dolphin leaped high out of the water. We could see the entire beach all the way back to our house.

"Dolphins been coming to these waters for thousands of years," said Delphis. "Fishing here was always good, least 'til humans started taking all the fish."

We glided in a long sweeping arc down to the sea. I felt dizzy, like I was on a roller coaster.

"You really are a magic dolphin!" Maria said.

"Told you I was," said Delphis.

"Awesome!" I said.

"Show us some more," said Maria.

Again we picked up speed, moving along the shoreline just beyond the surf zone. I had to tuck my legs under my body to keep my shoes dry. We were going so fast the wind blew Maria's hair back. We were both laughing.

Delphis slowed down to speak. His voice was high and squeaky, full of clicks and whistles and other strange dolphin sounds mixed in with words. We had to listen carefully to make sense of his scrambled speech.

"Where to, little friends?"

I was about to suggest a beach to the south where tons of fossil shark's teeth can be found. But Maria spoke first.

"Tell us about the lighthouse. Why is it in the middle of the sea?"

"Ah, yes," squeaked the dolphin. "The lighthouse (click, whistle) ... interesting story that (click, whistle, squeak)."

"Shake a fluke, friends. Here we go again!"

With a powerful slapping of his tail, Delphis leaped once more out of the water. This time he took us so high we were *above* the lighthouse. In the distance we could see Charleston Harbor. I closed my eyes, trying hard not to think about the pelicans skimming the sea below us. If my sister was nervous she didn't show it.

"That's the Morris Island Lighthouse," said Delphis. "The first lighthouse was blown up in the American Civil War. The one you see now was rebuilt on dry land behind the dunes."

"So, what's it doing in the water?" asked Maria.

"The beach moved," said Delphis.

"The beach moved?"

11

"Did. In fact, the entire beach retreated about a mile to the west," he explained. "Left the lighthouse in the sea."

We began a slow descent to the water. Cautiously I opened one eye, then the other. When we were safely floating again I felt relaxed enough to speak.

"No way," I protested. "Armies retreat, not beaches. A beach doesn't move! Uh ... does it?"

There followed a series of high-pitched squeaks that sounded exactly like human laughter.

Do dolphins have a sense of humor?

"How *can* a beach move?" asked Maria. "It's not like it's on wheels."

"No wheels required," clicked the dolphin. "Waves and currents took the beach sand from around the lighthouse and moved that sand somewhere else."

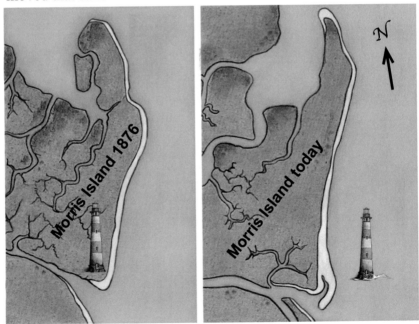

Since the 1870s the Morris Island beach has been moving west.

Maria looked thoughtful. "So the beach moved because of waves and currents. I guess that makes sense."

Delphis delivered a series of chirps, clicks and whistles sprinkled with English words, a grammatical mix that made no sense at all. *Must be hard being bilingual,* I thought. *Especially, when your native language is Dolphinese, or whatever it's called.*

But then he spoke with perfect clarity. "Beaches are among the most dynamic places on the planet," he said.

"What does 'dynamic' mean?" I asked.

"It means the beaches are always changing and moving, right?" answered Maria.

"Right. A big storm can move an entire beach in one day, though usually it takes months or years."

"Over time storms can even move whole islands," continued Delphis. "They call the process island migration."

"So the Morris Island beach really did move," I said.

"But the lighthouse stayed," said Maria.

"Geology at work," said Delphis.

"Like magic," I said.

"I'd like to know more about how waves and currents move beaches," said Maria.

"Me too," I said.

"That," said the dolphin, "is what I'm here for."

The beaches are moving !

13

The first year we lived at the beach was the happiest year of my life. I spent the summer swimming, fishing, collecting fossil shark's teeth or just hanging out on the beach with friends and family. Even when school was in session, there was time enough (after homework) for exploring. Time enough to play tag with the waves or scour the sand for the latest sea life tossed ashore by the whims of wind and tide. Life in those days was an endless holiday.

Then the storms came. Sometimes hurricanes made local landfalls, forcing us to evacuate and spend sleepless nights in motels on the mainland. Even storms that crept up the coast well offshore often sent monstrous waves our way that raged and roared and ripped up the beach, causing massive beach erosion. With each passing year the hurricanes seemed to become more powerful, more destructive and more frequent. Last night's storm was but the latest in a series of terrifying storms, so many in recent years that we learned to keep one eye on the sky and the other on the Weather Channel. At least during hurricane season.

The whooshing of air exhaling through a blowhole brought me back to the present. Looking across the water to our island, I could just make out the forest and some of the houses we had walked past. The air had that fresh, clean smell, like it always does after a storm. The wind was still gusty and storm clouds continued to jet their way toward the north. But the eastern sky was starting to clear.

Another beautiful day in paradise, I thought.

Yet, something was troubling me, something ominous swimming in the dark seas of my thoughts. *If the beaches are moving, that means …*

"Delphis," I asked anxiously. "The beach at our house. Is it moving?"

"Oh, yes," he answered. "It's eroding. In fact, your entire island will likely migrate toward the mainland, leaving your house stranded in the sea one day, just like the lighthouse."

"That's not exactly what we wanted to hear," I said.

"Sorry to be the bearer of bad news." Delphis issued a long mournful whistle.

"Is … is there nothing we can do to save our home?" Maria's voice was starting to crack.

"There is," said Delphis, after a long succession of whistles and clicks. "Learn how beaches work. Learn about the sea. Then you'll know what to do for your home."

"With knowledge," he continued, "comes power. And with power comes the ability to change things."

"All right," said Maria, with a new determination in her voice. "Tell us how beaches work!"

"Thought you'd never ask," said the dolphin, delivering a long, squeaky whistle. "To understand beaches you need to know about sea level rise."

We had drifted behind the lighthouse where the waves were smaller. I was grateful. It was difficult trying to understand a talking dolphin while at the same time concentrating on keeping my shoes out of the water.

Maria brushed hair back from her face. "There was something in the news recently about rising seas."

"Sea level rise is not exactly breaking news," said Delphis. "The ocean has been rising and falling for millions of years. During the last Ice Age the seas fell 400 feet (122 meters)."

"How come sea level went down in the Ice Age?" I asked.

Delphis answered with another question. "What happens to rain when it falls on land?"

"It goes into the rivers," I said.

"And the rivers empty into the sea," added Maria.

"Exactly," clicked Delphis. "Rainwater returns to the sea. Part of the water cycle, you know. But during an ice age the climate is cold (cold enough to freeze your flippers!). Rain falling on land turns to ice and never reaches the sea."

"I get it," Maria said. "The rainwater can't return to the sea. The amount of water in the ocean decreases. So sea level goes down."

"That pretty much sums it up," said Delphis. "During the last Ice Age sea level dropped so much that the shoreline was about 40 miles (64 kilometers) east of here. All this water around us was back then a forest full of mastodons and saber-toothed cats hunting sloths and giant armadillos."

"Imagine that." I laughed. "Saber-toothed cats and mastodons in South Carolina!"

"Then the world got warmer and the glaciers began to melt. The sea started to rise and the shoreline gradually retreated to its present location."

As Delphis spoke, I tried to imagine how the land must have

looked thousands of years ago. In my mind I saw a misty Ice Age forest, dark and mysterious and cold. Herds of enormous mastodons walked under snow-covered trees. Then the northern glaciers started melting. The sea, flooding with water from melting ice, rushed toward the forest. Waves broke against the trees. Year by year the forest was pushed back by the unstoppable sea. As the climate got warmer, the shoreline retreated. Ice Age mammals like mammoths and mastodons went extinct because they couldn't adapt to a changing climate.

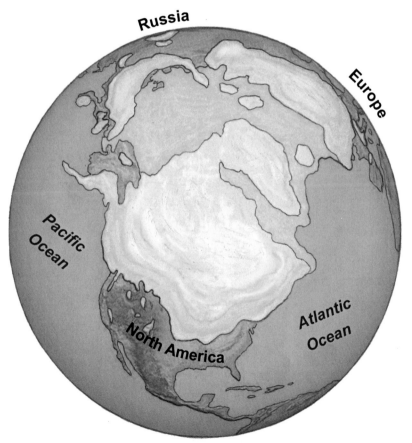

About 18,000 years ago, near the end of the last Ice Age, thick sheets of ice covered Canada and the northern parts of Europe, Russia and the United States.

Mastodons are the extinct relatives of mammoths and elephants. Sometimes people find the fossil remains of mastodons and other Ice Age mammals on beaches in the southeastern U.S.

Too bad about the mastodons, I thought. *It'd be so cool to see one walking down the beach. We could even have mastodon rides for the tourists.*

I had a sudden idea. "Is that why the beach at Morris Island moved back, because of sea level rise?"

"Good question," clicked Delphis. "The beach moved partly because of sea level rise. But the real cause was something that humans did to the beach."

I wanted to ask what people had done to the beach that caused it to shift, but Maria also had a question.

"Is sea level still rising?" she asked.

"Another good question," replied Delphis. "Little humans always ask great questions. Asking good questions is the first step toward doing science."

"Sea level is indeed still rising," said Delphis. "And it's rising fast. Won't be long before we dolphins will be swimming in the White House, holding underwater press conferences and having fish banquets for Congress!"

Delphis repeated the squeaks that sounded so much like human laughter. By now I was pretty sure he had a sense of humor.

"Just kidding," he said and then added, "Yep, the sea is still rising and the rate of sea level rise is speeding up. Glaciers everywhere are melting. You can really see it in a place like Greenland, where blocks of ice as big as houses fall into the sea."

"Ice cubes as big as a house," I said. "Ha, ha, ha! Boy, I'd like to see that!"

"You got it," said Delphis.

We began moving quickly away from land toward the open ocean.

"Hold on tight, little friends. Or should I call you little scientists? Here we go!"

And then off we went.

Sea level is rising.

hat happened next is hard to describe. One moment we were in the warm, sunny waters of South Carolina. Then everything got kind of "fuzzy" like a fog. I had a strange feeling as if an invisible hand was pushing me on an impossibly long swing. Wind tore at my hair. My stomach felt like it had been turned inside out.

Then the "fog" cleared and we found ourselves floating on a sea of ice. Everywhere I turned I saw ice. The whole world, it seemed, had become white.

But there was land too. We were off a coast where dark mountains rose above a long cliff of ice. And here and there black rocks stuck out from the ice.

Maria rubbed her eyes. "I've a feeling we're not in Carolina anymore."

"We're in Greenland," said Delphis.

"You've got to be joking!" I exclaimed.

"Love to make jokes," admitted Delphis. "But dolphin jokes and human jokes are different, you know. Anyhow, this is no joke. Little friends, welcome to Greenland."

"Arion, you did say you wanted to see big blocks of ice," recalled Maria.

"Did," agreed Delphis. "And Greenland is a good place to see blocks of ice. Here the ice falls and becomes icebergs. The icebergs melt and add their waters to the sea. Then voilà! You got sea level rise!"

We were silent for a moment, trying to make sense of what our dolphin guide had just said. It was warm and sunny. But I

could feel the cold seeping into my clothes from the icy water.

I pulled my legs up. Folded my arms. Maria did the same. We watched with amazement at countless icebergs, large and small, that littered the sea's surface like popcorn on a gray carpet.

"Greenland is one giant pile of ice (at least in the middle of the island). In places the ice is two miles (3 km) thick. Out from this mass of ice flow little glaciers like this one."

If this is a little glacier, what does a big one look like?

"It's so beautiful, so ..." Maria tried to find the right word.

"Awesome!" I said.

The Vikings settled in Greenland in the 10th century AD. From there they sailed to parts of North America, 500 years before Columbus.

21

"Speaking of awesome," said Delphis, licking his teeth. "The fishing here is pretty good! You guy's hungry? Nothing like a squirmy, crunchy fish to get a mammal going in the morning. Good source of protein and omega-3s, you know."

"No thanks," said Maria politely. "We already ate breakfast."

I never cared much for sushi (especially sushi that was still moving) and so said nothing.

"Pity," said Delphis, with what sounded like a hint of disappointment.

The ice cliff looked like something out of a fairy tale, a snow giant's castle, perhaps. Mostly it was creamy white, but in some places the ice glowed like veins of blue emeralds. And there were other colors as well — pinks and grays and purples and one small iceberg crowned yellow with a cluster of black dots.

Strange, I thought. *The dots on that iceberg just blinked.*

And then the whole iceberg moved.

"Holy moly"! I shouted. "Look!"

Spooked by the sound of my voice, a mother polar bear and her cub slipped off the berg into the water. We watched in

amazed silence as the two bears leisurely swam away, until disappearing into the distance.

"Polar bears need the ice to hunt seals," said Delphis. "As more polar ice melts in places like Greenland these bears will go hungry. They may even go extinct."

Polar bears going extinct because the polar ice was melting? I was skeptical. How could so much ice possibly melt?

"How do you know for sure the ice is melting?" I asked.

At that moment there came a rumble like a thunderstorm. A car-sized piece of the ice cliff broke off and splashed into the sea. It bobbed violently up and down for a few seconds. Then it flipped over and bumped against smaller icebergs, settled quietly in the water and sent ripples in our direction. We moved up and down with the ripples.

Maria laughed. "I guess that answers your question, Arion."

"Yeah, maybe," I said. "But why is the ice melting? It seems so cold here."

Delphis whistled. "Why does any ice melt? Why does snow melt in the spring?"

"Because the air temperature is warmer than the snow?" I asked.

"Exactly. And that's what's happening all around the world, you know. The atmosphere is getting warmer. The glaciers are melting. The meltwater flows into the sea."

"And sea level rises," said Maria.

"They call it global warming," said Delphis.

"Of course in winter," he continued, "snow falls on the glaciers, which adds more ice. But the Greenland ice is melting faster than it can be replaced by winter snow."

"And," he added, "it's caused by humans, you know."

"What do you mean?" asked Maria.

"Cars, planes and boats all run on fossil fuels, right? Burning fossil fuels (like gasoline) puts carbon dioxide into the atmosphere. Carbon dioxide, also known as CO_2 (see-oh-two), traps sunlight that might otherwise be reflected into space. The trapped sunlight heats up the air. The warmer air melts the world's glaciers."

"Everything in the world is connected," said Delphis, "like strands in a planet-sized fishing net."

I thought about what Delphis was saying. I'd heard about global warming before. Who hadn't? It was always on the news and we'd even talked about it at school. But I didn't know that humans were at fault. I didn't know polar bears were in trouble. And I didn't know global warming was causing sea level rise.

And sea level rise is threatening to wash our house away.

The weather began to change. A cold, biting wind, sharp as a shark's tooth, crept in from the west. Ghost-gray clouds devoured the sky. The sun, which had been lemon bright just moments ago, faded to a dusky orange and vanished into the gloom.

"Look at this ice," said Delphis. "If all the ice in Greenland were to melt, the ocean would rise more than 20 feet (6 m). Cities like New York and London would be flooded."

I rubbed my arms. The cold made it hard to concentrate, though our dolphin guide seemed unaffected.

"But melting ice is only half the story," he continued. "When water heats up it expands like a balloon. It's rather like ... (whistle, creak, click). Oh, I forgot the word. What do you call those things young humans ride? Two wheels. Starts with 'b' I think, yes?"

"You mean bicycles?" I said.

"That's it ... bicycles! Never actually rode one. But thank you for the word. It's like your bicycle tires in the summer. On a hot day the air in your tires expands and the tires get bigger. They feel more 'pumped up', don't they?"

"Th-that's right." My teeth were starting to chatter. I was wishing I'd brought a sweater.

"Same with oceans," concluded Delphis. "A hotter climate expands seawater (like pumped up bicycle tires) and sea level rises even more."

"It's getting chilly, Delphis. Can we go someplace warm?" Maria was blowing on her hands.

It was becoming windier and more overcast by the minute. The wind pelted us with tiny snowflakes. I was thinking about rising seas flooding the streets of New York and washing over smaller communities like ours. I was also thinking a little global warming on a cold day in Greenland might not be such a bad thing.

Then it happened again, the rumble of thunder, quiet at first and then increasingly louder. And it seemed to go on forever. Suddenly, the world in front of us exploded. A massive chunk of ice broke from the cliff and slid into the sea. It gathered momentum and when it hit the water a monstrous wave shot straight up, towering over our heads and blotting out the sky.

"Look out!" shouted Maria, covering her face with her hands.

I closed my eyes. I felt a rush of cold air as the wave engulfed us ...

We're in for it now! I thought.

But the wave never hit us. When I opened my eyes, we were high in the air. Far below, giant waves rolled out to sea, gradually getting smaller as they moved into deeper water. The chunk of ice, now an iceberg as long as a basketball court, had stabilized and was calmly resting on the sea as if it had always been there.

"Whoa! That was close!" I said. My heart was beating like a drum.

"Have no fear, friends," said Delphis. "By my flippers, no harm will ever come to you as long as you're with me."

I glanced down at my feet. I couldn't believe it. My shoes were still dry.

"Yes!" I said, grinning from ear to ear.

"Ready to move on?" asked Delphis.

"Definitely," I said.

"Absolutely," said Maria.

"As long as it's someplace warm," I added.

"You got it," said Delphis.

And off we went.

Sea level rise is caused by global warming, which melts glaciers and causes seawater to expand.

nce again everything became "foggy."
And once again my stomach seemed turned
inside out. But before I could ponder the
issue further, the fog cleared and we found
ourselves floating on a blue sea bordered by a long cliff as
white as any glacier. The cliff was topped with green fields and
houses and with what appeared to be a lighthouse. I reached
down to touch the water. It was cold but not nearly as cold as
the icy waters of Greenland.

"Where in the world are we, Delphis?" Maria asked.

"England," he answered, blowing a column of spray out his
blowhole. The spray drifted back with the wind and soaked our
faces.

"Sorry 'bout that."

"It's all right," I said, drying my face with my shirt.

Delphis pointed a flipper toward the shore.

"Those are the famed Cliffs of Dover," he said. "But we're
not here to talk about cliffs, you know."

Our guide whistled again. "Got other fish to fry," he said
and then "laughed."

I remembered reading about the Cliffs of Dover. They are
made of a soft rock called chalk, which formed millions of
years ago from the countless shells of tiny sea creatures. I was
hoping we'd stop so I could get a sample for my rock collec-
tion.

But Delphis had other plans.

Slapping his tail rapidly on the water, he started picking up
speed. Soon we were zipping over the waves as fast as a

powerboat. As we raced along the coast, staying close to the cliffs, a white ship approached from the north.

"What kind of boat do you think that is?" I asked Maria.

"Could be a fishing boat."

"Or a navy vessel," I said.

It was neither. As the ship got closer, we could make out the word "Ferry" written on its side. A crowd had gathered on the deck. Some of the passengers were waving their arms and pointing to something on the shore. Others were taking pictures. The excited voices of children floated across the water.

After the ferry had passed I asked Maria, "What were they pointing at?"

"Us, silly!"

"They must not get many kids riding dolphins in England," I joked.

"Ha, ha," said Maria.

The cliffs got smaller before disappearing entirely. The shore became a wide pebbly beach fringed by farms and houses, occasional trees and picturesque towns. In one of the towns stood an impressive stone building with circular towers. Banners fluttered in the breeze and people walked atop its outer wall.

"Look! Look! A castle!"

Maria was as excited as a gold miner who'd just unearthed a five-pound nugget. She craned her neck to better see. But we continued racing up the coast and the castle soon passed from view.

On a beach about a mile to the north stood a concrete wall, encasing piles of loose stones. The wall was roughly circular. The whole structure was not much bigger than a house.

Delphis slowed down to speak.

"We're near the town of Deal," he said. "This is one of several castles King Henry VIII built in the 16th century."

"This is a castle?" I said incredulously. "No way."

"Yes way," Delphis replied. "This is all that remains of Sandown Castle. What was once a proud fortress is now a pile of busted battlements and forgotten dreams."

"War?" asked Maria.

"The sea," replied Delphis.

"In those days humans didn't know about beach erosion. They built the castle too close to the ocean. Soon the waves began smashing its outer walls. Eventually, the sea punched through and the castle had to be abandoned."

"What'd they put a castle here for, anyway?" I wondered out loud.

Sandown Castle as it looked in the 1500s. The sea soon began eroding its outer walls.

"Defense," answered Delphis. "Invading armies have been landing here for thousands of years."

"It began with Julius Caesar, more than 2,000 years ago," he continued.

"I know about Caesar," said Maria, still studying the ruins of Sandown Castle. "We read the Shakespeare play in class last year."

"Then you probably know Caesar was an ambitious Roman general. Not satisfied with conquering most of Europe, he wanted England as well. So he sailed across the English Channel with his army and landed somewhere near here. The Romans pulled their ships up on the beach and charged into the hills to fight the Britons. That was what the tribes living here were called, you know."

"But Caesar didn't know much about tides (a serious deficiency for a naval commander). Caesar didn't know tides are higher under a full moon. Imagine his surprise when he returned to find his ships flooded by the full-moon tide and smashed to splinters by the waves."

"Everybody knows about spring tides," said Maria.

31

Julius Caesar looking in dismay at his wrecked fleet. Caesar didn't know that higher than normal tides (called spring tides) occur during a full moon (and also during a new moon).

"Everybody but Caesar, it would seem," I said.

"Caesar learned a valuable lesson that day. No one commands the sea, not even a great general!"

"Does that mean we can't stop the sea from taking our house?" Maria asked. "You told us if we learned how beaches work, we could save our house."

"That's right," I added. "You did say that."

For a while nobody spoke. All was quiet save for wind and waves.

Delphis swam in an ever-widening circle, now and then whooshing air through his blowhole. It seemed to me that he was thinking about something. *Perhaps he hadn't heard us,* I thought.

At last he gave a hawk-like whistle and spoke, "I said if you learn how beaches work and learn about the sea, then you'll know what to do for your home, right?"

"Tell you what, little friends," he continued. "Will make a deal with you. Teach you what to do for your home. In return, I have a small favor to ask."

"What kind of favor?" Maria asked cautiously.

"Nothing you would not want to do anyway. And nothing too troublesome."

"All right," said Maria. "It's a deal."

"Ha, ha, ha!" I laughed. "It's a deal at Deal!" Then I remembered how scary last night's storm had been. I stopped laughing. Like my sister, I too was eager to learn how to keep the sea from taking our home.

"First, there's something I want you to see. We'll just 'coast' along the shoreline a while," he said. "Get it?"

And then Delphis laughed, cackling like a coven of witches on Halloween night.

By this time we had drifted closer to the beach. Maria looked up and down the shore. "I don't see anything unusual. I see a pier with some fishermen, but piers are common on beaches, at least in the Carolinas."

"I think I see another castle."

"Where?" said Maria excitedly.

"Keep looking," said Delphis.

I studied the sky and the sea. I observed the clouds. I watched the houses slowly going by. *Of course, the houses are going by. That means...*

"Hey," I said. "We're moving!"

"Ah, good, little friend," said Delphis. "Now tell us why."

"It's some kind of current," Maria announced.

"Bravo! You both get an A for the day. We're moving because of the longshore current. Most shorelines have a longshore current. You've probably felt it before and didn't even know it."

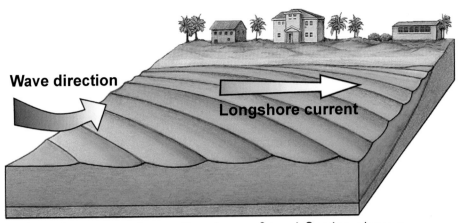

Wave direction

Longshore current

Longshore currents are like rivers of sand flowing along a shoreline. They are caused by waves, which in turn are caused by the wind.

"I remember a day when the waves were really big, but we went swimming anyway," said Maria. "We jumped in the water and before we realized it, we had drifted far down the beach. Was that because of the longshore current?"

"Was," said Delphis. "The longshore current carried you down the shore. It also carries sand along a shoreline. Longshore currents are like rivers of sand flowing from beach to beach."

Several minutes passed. The current took us further down the coast. We bobbed up and down with the waves, a motion that soon made me sleepy. I leaned my head on my sister's shoulder and closed my eyes. I likely would have fallen asleep and toppled into the water if Maria hadn't spoken.

"Hey!" she cried. "What happened to the beach?"

I opened my eyes. The beach was gone. In front of us stretched a rock wall, stained green-brown by the sea. Plastic bottles and other trash sloshed back and forth in the surf and clunked noisily against the wall. A trio of seagulls, perched like sentinels on the wall, regarded us suspiciously. Beyond the wall stood some houses.

"What are we looking at?" I asked.

"A seawall," answered Delphis. "Humans made it to protect their houses from beach erosion. This one is made of rocks. But I've seen seawalls made of concrete, wood and sandbags. And once, years ago in Australia, I swam by a seawall made of old cars."

"We need to get one for our house," I said half seriously.

"That's it!" Maria said excitedly. "We could build a seawall in front of the dunes! Then storm waves can't touch our house!"

"Is that right, Delphis?" I asked. "A seawall would protect our house?"

"Would," he said. "For a while."

Seawalls destroy beaches. The seawall in front of the house on the left caused the beach to erode away. The house on the right has no seawall and so still has a beach.

"Yes!" Maria happily proclaimed.

"Finally!" I said. "We found the answer."

"Let's go back now and tell Mom and Dad."

"But seawalls have a problem." Delphis issued a mournful whistle that began as a high note and ended several octaves lower.

Uh-oh, here comes the catch, I thought.

"Seawalls destroy beaches."

"Once a nice sandy beach stretched along this shore. Little humans played in the sand with their moms. Parent humans fished from the beach. Then they put up a seawall. Waves and the longshore current began taking the sand away. Eventually, the beach vanished. Will happen on your island too if a seawall gets built."

"What if our seawall is made of sandbags?" Maria asked.

"Same result," replied Delphis.

"What if it's made of granite boulders?" I asked.

"Same," said Delphis. "Build a seawall and say goodbye to the beach! Seawalls protect houses but destroy beaches."

"That's what happened to Sandown Castle," he explained. "The castle's outer wall acted like a seawall. Caused the beach to erode. No sand was left to slow down the waves. The sea ate that castle, swallowed it whole and spit the rubble out."

Maria and I were silent. Delphis whistled and squeaked and then said, "There's another way, another structure that'll protect your house *and* keep the beach in place. Guess you'll be wanting to see it, I suppose."

"Show us," Maria said simply.

Once again we sped along the coast, bouncing over the waves like a skipping rock.

This time we went back toward Deal. We slowed when we reached two houses overlooking the sea. Between the houses stood a line of rocks, sticking straight out into the water. There are similar structures in South Carolina, some even on our island. I'd seen them but never paid them any attention.

"These rocks were not made by the sea," said Delphis. "Humans put them there. The structure is called a groin. Notice how sand piles up on one side of the groin but not the other?"

"The house on the left has a wide beach in front of it," said Maria.

"But the house on the right has no beach at all," I observed.

"So, what happened to the beach on the right?" asked Maria.

"Maybe the groin caused the beach to vanish," I suggested.

"Good," said Delphis. "But why?"

I was thinking hard. "You said longshore currents carry sand along the beach, right?"

"I did."

"And that a longshore current is like a river of sand."

"That's it!" exclaimed Maria. "The rocks must have stopped the flow of sand."

"Correct," said Delphis. "Sand is food for a beach. If anything blocks the supply of sand, the beach starves. It gets skinny. If it gets too skinny, it disappears."

"Groins trap sand," he continued. "The longshore current piles sand on one side of the groin and the beach there gets wider. But the other side is starved of sand. There the beach gets narrow."

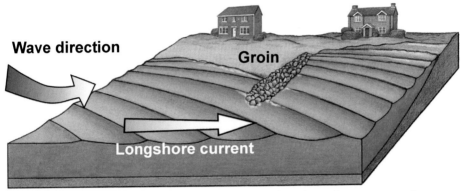

Groins control beach erosion by blocking the longshore current. This causes sand to pile up on one side of the groin, which widens the beach and protects houses at that location. But the longshore current removes sand from the other side of the groin, causing erosion further down the beach.

"You could build a groin in front of your house," he said. "You'd have a nice wide beach to protect your house from storm waves. But your neighbor's house might have no beach at all."

"It wouldn't be fair," said Maria, "to widen the beach in front of our house but take sand away from our neighbor's beach. I guess groins are no good for beaches."

I thought about our neighbor standing in the ruins of his deck. Maria was right. Constructing a groin in front our house would not be a "neighborly" thing to do.

We drifted close to the tip of the groin, where it dipped below the water. Waves made slurping sounds as the sea slipped in and out of the barnacle-encrusted rocks.

Delphis whistled. By now we understood this was his way of announcing he had something important to say.

"You know why barnacles never give money to charity?"

"Barnacles never give money to charity?" I was confused. "What ...?"

"Because they're shellfish."

There followed a long minute of silence. Finally Maria said, "Delphis, was that a joke?"

"Was," he said.

Then I got it. "Ha, ha, ha," I laughed. "Good one."

"Thanks. I'm working on my interspecies humor. Not as easy as it sounds, you know."

Just below the water's surface something small and white caught my eye. I reached over and picked it up. It was a rock.

"Yes!" I cried.

"What is it?" asked Maria.

"Chalk from the Cliffs of Dover," I said. "Probably carried here by waves."

Beaming widely, I put the specimen in my pack.

"Another gift from the sea," said Maria.

Delphis turned his head and looked up toward the sun, now high in the sky.

"Getting late, friends. Time we move on."

We began moving out to sea away from the shore.

"But 'cause you are such good students, we'll hit another beach for shell collecting. Find some rocks. Maybe even a fossil or two. Or perhaps young humans are homesick and wish to return home, I guess."

"No way!" I said. "I'm ready for another beach."

"Me too," said Maria. "Especially if the shell hunting is good."

"Outstanding!" said Delphis. "Buckle up. Next stop is Africa!"

And off we went.

Nobody commands the sea!

Sea walls and groins protect houses but destroy beaches.

5 **Beach Robbers**

By now we were used to the near-instantaneous transition from one beach to another. When the fog cleared, we found ourselves just inches above the water, racing madly over a boundless blue sea, chasing waves rolling to an unknown shore somewhere beyond the next horizon. Every time it seemed certain we would slam savagely into the back of a wave, Delphis slapped the water with his tail and kept us safely airborne.

The wind blew Maria's hair straight back into my eyes. I had to lean sideways to see where we were going.

"This is so cool!" she shouted.

"Like Aladdin on his magic carpet!" I shouted back.

Spreading my arms like the wings of a gull, I stood up and closed my eyes. Then I thought better of it. We were moving so fast even a magic dolphin might find it hard to pluck a kid out of the water if he fell. I'd be like Icarus after his wings melted.

We smelled land before we saw it. The wind carried odors that reminded me of campfires and something similar to the olive oil Mom uses for cooking. But there were other curious, unknown smells as well. Some were exotically sweet like jasmine, others not so pleasant.

The shore was closer than we first realized. Wrapped in a blanket of brown haze, it had been hidden from view. Soon the outlines of a splendid white city on a hill emerged from the haze. Towers graced its skyline and palm trees lined its water-front. Sheltered within a rocky breakwater, colorful fishing boats painted red and blue and green floated peacefully in the harbor. From across the water we heard the rustle and roar of a modern city — the muffled sounds of traffic, horns blaring, people shouting, the cries of school children. In the distance a male singer's melodic, high-pitched voice rang out from a loudspeaker.

"Prayer time," said Delphis.

I remembered an illustration from *The Arabian Nights*, one of the books Dad used to read to us when we were young. The city looked like the kind of place Sinbad the Sailor might have visited. *Perhaps Sinbad brought his ship here for repairs after battling fierce sea monsters.*

42

"Where are we?" asked Maria.

Delphis slowed down as we approached the harbor. Head-lands protected us from the big rollers we'd seen earlier. Here the swells were choppy but small.

"Morocco," he said. "At the city of Larache (Luh - rosh)."

Maria was inspecting the buildings, no doubt trying to classify the architectural styles.

"Some of the buildings look really old," she noted.

"Old?" said Delphis. "Very. The Phoenicians (Fuh-**knee**-shins) settled here about 2,500 years ago."

"Wow!" I said. "And I thought Charleston was old!"

"The Phoenicians chose their site well," continued Delphis. "They built their city upriver on a hill where sea level rise would not be a problem."

The Phoenicians were a seafaring people from what is today called Lebanon.

There followed a series of squeaks, whistles and other peculiar dolphin sounds.

"If you live near the sea," Delphis advised, "live on high ground. And away from the water!"

"That's not an option for us," said Maria.

"We live in the low country," I explained.

"And right next to the sea," Maria added.

Maybe right in the sea if another big storm comes our way, I thought.

Larache overlooks a river that meanders past the harbor. On the opposite bank, across from the city, a fisherman had hauled his boat onto land and was painting a blue dolphin on the bow. A boy was sitting on the dolphin's back.

That's kind of weird, I thought.

So absorbed was the fisherman in his work that he didn't even look up as we glided by.

I thought we would continue up the river to where the ruins of the Phoenician city lay, but instead Delphis took us back to the sea. Leaving the harbor behind, we followed a wide sandy beach, topped by the biggest dunes I had ever seen.

The country consisted of brown hills dotted with olive trees (according to Delphis) and with cork trees (a kind of oak). It was pretty country, though not as green as England.

"I don't suppose you kids brought any fish with you, did you yes?" said Delphis, between clicks and whistles.

"Forgot to pack the fish," I said.

"Too bad. Sea journeys always make me hungry. We could go fishing together?"

"Thanks," said Maria. "But I'm not hungry."

"Me neither," I said. Then I remembered our poor dolphin friend probably hadn't eaten breakfast. I wondered how long he'd been stranded on the beach without food.

"Delphis, why don't you fish while we look for shells on the beach?" I suggested.

Licking his teeth, Delphis replied, "You hunt shells. I hunt fish. That'll work. But stay close to the water. If trouble comes I cannot help you on land."

Apparently a magic dolphin's powers end at the water's edge.

"Sounds like a plan," said Maria.

"Let's do it," I agreed.

Delphis wiggled, squirmed and bounced his way onto the beach. Maria and I hopped off. Unfortunately, my timing was poor and I jumped right onto an incoming wave. My shoes were now hopelessly wet. *Bad luck,* I thought. *Mom's not going to be happy.*

"Back in 20 minutes," said Delphis, as he slid away from the shore. "Remember, stay close to the water!"

"Happy fishing," I said.

It felt good to stretch our legs but it was kind of lonesome without Delphis. We watched him slip gracefully through the surf. Disappearing beneath a wave, he'd reappear seconds later with a fish in his mouth, which he always swallowed in one gulp.

"Must be fun to be a dolphin," said Maria.

"Only if you like raw fish," I noted.

"Well, at least the fish is always fresh."

"Bet I'll find more shells than you," I challenged.

"You're on."

Shells there were a plenty. But finding quality shells turned out to be difficult. Tire tracks ran up and down the beach in all directions and almost every shell we found had been broken or crushed by whoever had driven on the beach. Some were cracked like a jigsaw puzzle. They looked whole, but when we picked them up they fell apart in our hands. We decided to walk a little higher on the beach where there were fewer tire tracks.

The wind was so annoying! Frequent gusts blasted sand into our eyes, forcing us to turn our faces toward the sea. Without realizing it, we began straying farther from the water where the wind was not so fierce. Before long we were right next to the dunes, at a considerable distance from the shore.

"Let's climb to the top," I said.

"Delphis told us to stay close to the water."

"Ah, come on. Just for a minute. We can see the city better from up there. Might see some cool buildings. Maybe even an old castle."

That convinced her.

"Okay. But just for a minute."

We followed some tire tracks that curled like a lizard's tail through a gap in the dunes. The trail was steep and we were soon breathing heavily. Just before we reached the top we heard the whine of an engine.

"What is it?" asked Maria.

"Sounds like a plane," I said.

"Or a truck."

"Whatever it is, it's getting closer."

Suddenly a gigantic dump truck flew over the crest of the dune right in front of us. It seemed to leap in the air over our heads, splattering sand in all directions. I got a glimpse of two wheels and an axle and then the truck bore down on us. There was no time to do anything except jump out of the way. Maria leaped to one side of the trail and I to the other.

As the truck roared by, I glanced up at the driver, a young, dark-haired man wearing sunglasses. Loud music blasted from an open window. The man shook his fist at me and shouted a stream of words in a language I didn't understand. Then he was gone.

"Are you all right, Arion?" Maria asked.

"Okay. And you?"

"I'm all right, but I think we should go back to the water."

"Definitely," I agreed.

When Maria gets angry she folds her arms and stomps her feet. She was stomping and folding now.

"That guy should not be driving so fast!" she said, with great indignation. "He almost ran us down!"

"Must be late for a doctor's appointment," I ventured.

More stomping. "Argh!"

With the wind at our backs, we slid down the face of the dune like a pair of cross-country skiers. I was sweating, not only from the exertion of climbing but also from the realization that we'd come close to getting run over. The truck was now far down the beach, where it joined a cluster of other trucks. In my agitated imagination, they looked like a herd of grazing mastodons.

Delphis was waiting for us at the water's edge. "No problems?"

Maria related the incident with the dump truck.

"Ah, beach robbers!" said Delphis.

"Robbers!" I exclaimed.

"Was afraid they might still be here. That's why I said to stay near the water."

Delphis turned around so that his flukes were resting on the sand. "Climb aboard," he said, laughing his dolphin laugh. "I'll show you their hideout!"

I didn't think it was such a good idea to get close to a bunch of robbers, especially after the close call with the dump truck. But before I could say anything, Delphis took us straight out to sea and then sped along the coast to where the "herd" of trucks had gathered. From the water we could see men busily shoveling sand into the backs of the trucks. Sometimes a gust of wind intercepted a shovelful of tossed sand and carried it toward the surf. The air around the trucks was heavy with dust and diesel fumes.

"What are they doing?" I asked.

"Taking sand from the beach," Delphis answered. "What is known as beach mining."

"But what do they want so much sand for?" I asked.

"Morocco has few forests to provide lumber, so most buildings are made of bricks or concrete. They use the sand to make the concrete," Delphis explained.

"Beach mining is a big industry here, you know," he continued. "Good for business. Bad for the beach."

"Why is that?" asked Maria.

"Remember what you learned about beaches in England, yes?"

"Uh ... let's see." I tried to recall our visit to Deal. "You said sand is food for a beach."

"And seawalls and groins starve the beach of sand," added Maria.

"And then the beach erodes and gets skinny," I said.

"And maybe even disappears," concluded Maria.

"You remember well. Same with beach mining. Like seawalls and groins, beach mining starves the beach of sand."

The wind shifted in our direction, bringing with it the sharp, pungent odor of diesel fumes.

"It smells bad too," I said, holding my nose.

"Does," agreed Delphis.

Whistling loudly, he continued, "But there's more. And it's important, right? So listen carefully!"

"A beach is not just a bunch of waves pushing sand grains around. A beach is a living community of plants and animals. Scientists call a community like that an ecosystem. Shellfish, crabs, insects, and critters too small to see, all live in beach sand. Turtles lay their eggs on the beach. Birds nest on the beach and find their food there. Even land animals sometimes come down to the beach to munch on snacks."

"Mining beach sand," continued Delphis, "takes away an important food source and nesting ground for all kinds of animals. How would you feel if robbers broke into your house and stole your food?"

"I wouldn't like it," Maria said.

"Me neither. I'd be angry."

"Now I see why you called them beach robbers," said Maria. "They aren't just taking sand. They are robbing the beach of its life."

"Exactly. And beach mining not only hurts life, it also destroys the natural beauty of a beach. Is there anything more beautiful than a natural beach?"

"Aside from a school of fresh, tasty fish. Or some of the lady dolphins I met in the South Pacific," Delphis added as an afterthought.

"Is it okay to take just a little sand from the beach?" I asked. "Like if a kid needed sand to play with?"

I was thinking about the time when Dad loaded his pickup with beach sand for our sand box.

"If everyone takes even a little bit of beach sand," answered Delphis, "that adds up to a lot of sand over time, right?"

"A nice, wide, sandy beach," he continued, "makes for a healthy ecosystem."

"And," he said, with a series of clicks and whistles, "it also protects your house from storms. Take away the sand and storms will take away your house."

"That makes sense," said Maria. "A wide beach would slow down storm waves."

"Keep the beach natural and everybody's happy. Birds are happy. Turtles are happy. Persons are happy."

Delphis nodded his head rapidly while clicking and whistling. "And dolphins are happy 'cause there are lots of juicy, tasty fish to eat!"

"That reminds me. Know why the dolphin crossed the channel?"

"Uh ... to get to the other side?" I said.

"You heard that one?" Delphis sounded surprised.

"Just a lucky guess," I answered.

By this time we had drifted to a point directly downwind from the trucks. The stink of diesel fumes was too much. I felt like I was going to throw up. I started to gag.

"I think I'm going to be sick. Can we go someplace else, please?"

"Yeah," echoed Maria. "A beach with no dump trucks!"

"I know just the place. 'Seas' the day, little friends! Here we go."

And off we went.

Beach mining starves a beach of sand, robs a beach of its life and makes beach houses more likely to be damaged by storms.

y sister loves cities. And crowds. She likes to hang out at the beach with her friends, especially where there's a miniature golf course nearby. Her idea of paradise is a beach that's so crowded you can hardly find a place to sit and when sunbathing gets tiresome there's a mall conveniently close for window-shopping.

Yuck! I like my beaches wild. No people. No stores, just the primitive purity of sand and sea and sun. I always dreamed of being like Robinson Crusoe, exploring my very own private beach far from civilization on a shore full of exotic wildlife.

I was about to get my wish. But as Mom always says, "Be careful of your wishes, for they may come true!"

As usual, Mom was right.

Once again we were racing across the sea, this time down a coast blanketed by fog as thick as day-old oatmeal. Sometimes the fog thinned enough to offer an enchanting glimpse of empty beaches, dunes and low sandy hills. Not a house, not even a tree in sight. But mostly the fog was so dense we could see nothing at all. At those moments it seemed we were the only life on a watery planet whose vast oceans rolled to infinity.

Along a stretch of coast where the fog had lifted somewhat, Delphis took us closer to shore. The thunder of waves pounding sand filled our ears. The air was so dense with fog and spray that our noses were dripping water.

The surf here must be huge, I thought.

In the distance a solitary shape emerged from the mist like an outcrop of dark stone. But as we got closer, I saw it was too symmetrical to be anything natural. It looked more like a ...

"A ship!" shouted Maria. "Look, a shipwreck!"

And so it was, some kind of freighter, tossed up on the sand like a lump of iron driftwood.

"I'll bet it ran aground in the fog," I said.

"The coast here is hard and hungry and shows no mercy," said Delphis. "A shoreline littered with the skeletons of wrecked ships and the bones of marooned sailors. They call this place the Skeleton Coast."

"The Skeleton Coast." Maria shivered. "Sounds spooky."

"We're off the coast of Namibia in southwest Africa," said Delphis. "One of the driest deserts on the planet. Hundreds of miles of beaches with no humans and no towns."

"Beautiful," I said.

"But there's nothing here," said Maria, shaking her head.

"I like it," I said. "This is what beaches are supposed to look like."

"Yep," said Delphis after his usual volley of clicks and squeaks. "I wanted to show you a natural beach not yet spoiled by persons."

"And also," Delphis slowed until we were barely moving, "to pose a question."

"What question?" said Maria.

The dolphin whistled like a hawk and said, "What will happen to this coast when sea level rises?"

I thought for a moment. "Well, I guess that ship will be covered by the sea. Or maybe it will get pushed further up the beach."

"Let's put the question another way," he said. "What's the difference between sea level rise here and where you live?"

"Oh, that's easy," I replied. "Where we live, the rising sea will flood our house."

"So, what about here?"

"I'm not sure what you mean," I said.

"I think I see his point, Arion. Delphis is saying sea level rise isn't a problem here because there are no houses to be flooded."

"That's right." Delphis made a sound like a door turning on rusty hinges. "When the ocean rises on the Skeleton Coast, the beach will move into the desert. The beach critters will not care. They'll retreat with the beach. And the birds will not care. They'll just follow the beach critters."

"And the humans won't care 'cause no humans live here!" Delphis laughed a long, squeaky, click-filled laugh.

"Sea level rise," he continued, "is not a problem for the life that lives on a natural beach. But it is a problem for humans living in houses near the shore!"

"But just about everyone lives near the shore!" protested Maria. "I mean ... except for here. Millions of people live on the coast. We live at the beach. We can't just pick up our house and move away from the rising sea."

"Maybe," Delphis replied. "But there are communities in the world that do just that. They pick up their houses and move them back with the rising sea."

Maria looked thoughtful. "I'd like to see that," she said.

"Can do," said Delphis, turning to examine the sun high in the African sky. "But we'll have to swim fast if I'm to get you home before lunch."

But I was not ready to leave yet. I wanted to explore the shipwreck, so tantalizingly close across the water. I felt the ship plucking my heartstrings like a siren. I just had to see it.

"Delphis, can't we visit the shipwreck, please?"

"Time and tide wait for no one, little friend. Not even for a magic dolphin. Best move on."

But by now I'd learned well the art of dolphin persuasion.

"I imagine the fishing here must be good, perhaps even outstanding," I observed almost casually.

Delphis responded with a long whistle.

"Hmm ... fish," he said, licking his teeth. "You're not trying to tempt me to stay longer, are you little friend?"

"Wouldn't think of it," I said innocently. "Just ten minutes. We'll walk once around the ship and then leave, okay?"

"Ten minutes. But promise you'll stay near the water."

"Promise," I said for both of us.

"Hold fast. This might be a bit tricky."

Delphis took us toward the surf. The water became rougher and the sound of breaking waves boomed ever louder. The shore vanished from sight as we slipped into a wave trough. The next wave picked us up and for a brief moment we were perched on the crest of a mountain of water, looking straight down the face of a 30-foot (9 m) watery cliff.

We started falling. Wind ripped through my hair like a hurricane. I closed my eyes ... and screamed.

This was a totally bad idea! We're going to die for sure!

But nothing happened. When I opened my eyes, we were
surfing across the side of a monster wave so big it seemed to
reach all the way to the sky.

The wave curled over us, slowly compressing into a dark
tunnel. After a long minute, light started filtering from above,
transforming the tunnel into liquid emerald. I reached out and
touched the water. Felt it streaming through my fingers.

Magic, I thought.

We shot out of the tunnel like a rocket. The wave seemed to break everywhere at once, exploding in a white fury of foam and soupy spray. With powerful thrusts of his flukes, Delphis kept us in front of the foam. Kept us dry.

We rode the wave all the way to the beach, right up to the ship's stern. Then the wave hissed out to sea and Maria and I hopped safely onto the sand.

"Wow! Let's do that again!"

"No thank you!" Maria replied. "Once is enough!"

"Ten minutes," said Delphis. "Stay near the ship and have care. Other beasties than crabs and seabirds prowl these shores. And some may not be so friendly to young humans."

"We'll be careful," I said.

The sand was so wet we decided to carry our shoes and explore barefoot. It was probably an average-sized vessel, but standing upright on the beach completely out of the water, the ship towered over our heads. Its sides were badly rusted and when we touched the hull, chunks of plating peeled off and crumbled in our hands. The wind moaned like a ghost through jagged holes where the steel had rusted through. Peering into a hole, I spotted armies of fearsome crabs scuttling through the dark, sand-filled interior. The entire vessel reeked of salt and rotting seaweed and other unidentifiable sea smells.

I don't know what I expected to find. Gold coins maybe or the bones of shipwrecked sailors. But there was not much to see. Even the ship's name had rusted away. It took us less than five minutes to walk around the entire wreck. I was disappointed.

But then I noticed another dark shape, partly concealed in the fog further down the beach.

"Look!" I shouted. "Another shipwreck!"

"Uh-uh," Maria said. "No way we are leaving this spot. We don't know what's out there."

But I was already running toward what was sure to be another ruined ship waiting to be explored. *Just a quick sprint down the beach and I'll be back in time for our rendezvous with Delphis.*

I was almost to my objective when I stopped in my tracks. The thing on the beach had indeed been washed ashore. But it was not a ship. It was not anything even remotely human made. It was, in fact, a beached whale, partly buried in the sand, bloated and stinking with decay. Waves washed over a fluke. And around its sides and on top were dark shapes moving in the mist.

To my horror the shapes resolved themselves into lions.

Lions feeding on a whale. This can't be real!

I heard Maria run up behind me.

"Holy moly!" she said in a hoarse whisper. "Lions! Back to the ship, now!"

But my legs had turned to stone. I was caught in a perilous no-man's-land between fear and fascination. Part of me wanted to flee, to escape, but the other part wanted to get closer, to observe nature in its raw, brutal simplicity.

And so I did nothing. I stayed where I was, even as one of the lions, a large male, jumped onto the sand and started walking toward us.

Maria grabbed my arm. "Run!" she screamed.

We ran. I glanced over my shoulder. Mercifully, the lions were not following. They remained unmoving like statues, clustered around the dead whale.

We reached the shipwreck.

"Boy, that was close!" I laughed, my heart pounding wildly.

Maria was not laughing. "You're always getting us into trouble, Arion! Why can't you follow directions?"

"How was I to know lions were on the beach?"

"Just once I wish you'd do what you're told to do."

"All right, all right," I said, trying to sound contrite. "I will."

Something felt wrong. I glanced around.

"No," I said. "We have to go back!"

"What are you talking about?" Maria asked.

I pointed to my shoeless feet. "I must have dropped my sneakers when we were running," I said, trying to hold back tears. "We have to go back."

I looked down the beach toward the whale, but the fog had returned. I could see nothing.

"We are not going anywhere near those lions," Maria said firmly.

She was right, of course. There was nothing to do.

At least I don't have to worry anymore about keeping my shoes dry, I thought wryly.

At that moment Delphis appeared, two fish hanging out of his mouth. He swallowed the fish and smoothly surfed up to the beach. We climbed on his back.

And off we went.

As a shoreline retreats, the non-human beach life does the same (at least on a natural beach).

7 Tsunami

We slipped across a dark sea as smooth as polished slate, leaving a wake that bubbled and glowed in the light of a full moon. Stars were everywhere, sparkling like 4th of July fireworks in the sky above and reflecting in the sea around us. We were on a spaceship blasting through a watery galaxy, or so it seemed to my excited imagination.

Moonlight on an open sea. It was an enchanting scene, or would have been but for one important detail. The sea was full of garbage! Bottles, lumber, cans, glass fishing floats, wooden doors, upturned boats, cardboard boxes and plastic in a zillion shapes, colors and sizes dipped and bobbed and floated on the sea. We even passed a motorcycle, though how it was floating I couldn't say. It was as if a million garbage trucks had dumped their loads at the same spot in the ocean.

I studied my reflection, dancing on the ripples made by our passing. Small bits of plastic drifted on the surface. Even far below in the depths of the moon-soaked water I could see suspended debris.

"Where did all this trash come from?" asked Maria.

Delphis slowed down. "We're at the edge of the Great Pacific Garbage Patch," he said. "Here the world's garbage gathers and circles the ocean forever."

"But ... but where did the trash come from?" I said, repeating Maria's question.

"Humans."

"Which humans?" Maria wanted to know.

"Humans on beaches, in cities, on rivers, on ships, on roads. Humans all over the world throw their trash away. Winds and currents carry the trash to the middle of the sea."

"That puts a whole new perspective on littering," said Maria.

"Does," agreed Delphis. "But the big trash comes from a tsunami."

"Sue who?" asked Maria.

"Tsunamis," I explained, never shy about showing off my knowledge, "are giant waves caused by undersea earthquakes, landslides or even asteroids striking the ocean."

"Correct," whistled Delphis. "When a tsunami comes ashore, it knocks down everything in its path — cars, trees, buildings. And when it goes back out to sea, it carries the wreckage with it. The big trash here is from a tsunami that hit Japan."

Nobody spoke as we zigzagged our way around endless islands of trash. I was thinking of the terrifying images we had seen on the news about the recent Japanese tsunami.

A good reason not to live on the coast, I thought. *At least on one with earthquakes.*

We skirted a particularly large mound of garbage. I spotted something out of the corner of my eye.

"Wait! Hold it! Stop!" I cried. "Turn around!"

"Problem?"

"Go back, please," I said. "I think I saw something."

Delphis made a long lazy arc, retracing our passage.

"A little to the left. That's it. Right here. Stop."

On top of the mound, sandwiched between a pair of rusted oil cans, was the object of my interest. Two objects really. Leaning over, I picked them up.

"Yes!" I said, pumping my fist. "Just my size."

"Size?" said Delphis.

Maria explained how I'd left my shoes on the Skeleton Coast.

"Now it seems Arion has found a pair of sneakers to replace the ones he lost."

"My lucky day!" I proclaimed. Except for the salty laces, the shoes looked brand new. They fit perfectly.

"One person's good luck is another's misfortune," said Delphis. The sneakers no doubt belonged to a Japanese youth 'bout your age."

That dampened my enthusiasm. *Did the kid survive the tsunami?* I wondered.

"You'll be lucky indeed," noted Maria, "if you can explain to Mom how you left the house with red shoes and returned wearing white ones."

"I'll think of something," I said.

"You always do," she answered.

Delphis blasted a long column of spray out his blowhole. Luckily, the breeze carried the spray away.

"Stopped here to rest. Carrying persons across oceans is hard work!"

"I guess even a magic dolphin needs a break," said Maria.

"Got that right," he said. "Also wanted to show you the consequences of littering. When land trash washes out to sea, it can cause much mischief."

From now on, I'll be more careful about littering, I thought.

"Of course, sea level rise will just make the problem worse."

"How so?" asked Maria.

"The rising sea will wash over the land like a slow-moving tsunami. Tides and waves and currents will grab everything in the way (including trash) and pull it all out to sea. More trash, more plastic will pile up in the world's oceans."

"I don't mean to scare anyone," interrupted Maria. "But something big is moving in the water."

In the moonlight I could make out a dark triangle knifing through the sea about 100 feet (30 m) in front of us.

"It's a shark!" I cried.

"No," said Maria. "It's not a shark. It's a sea turtle."

And so it was. A turtle as big as a man, with jagged ridges running down a barnacle-crowned back like some kind of pre-historic sea monster. Every so often a massive flipper paddled the water, sending out concentric rings of ripples. But its head could not be seen, for it was completely enveloped in plastic.

"Poor animal!" exclaimed Maria. "It's tangled in a plastic bag. Hold my hand, Arion. I'm going to pull that bag off."

"Careful of its jaws!" I warned.

Delphis swam alongside the turtle. Maria reached over and tugged at the bag. But it was wrapped too tightly and all she succeeded in doing was to tighten the plastic's grip, threatening to strangle the poor creature.

"Here, try this." I opened my pocketknife.

With a few deft strokes, she sliced the plastic enough that it slipped off the turtle's neck and floated away.

The turtle tilted its head and solemnly regarded us for a long moment. A dark, wrinkled eye blinked as if to say, "Thanks, young humans." Then the animal lumbered away and sank into the silent depths.

"Well done, friends. Your good deed for the day."

"Second good deed for the day," I pointed out.

"What was the first?"

"We freed a stranded dolphin."

Delphis "laughed."

"How does a turtle get trapped in plastic?" said Maria.

"Happens a lot," said Delphis. "To a sea turtle, plastic bags look like jellyfish, a favorite food for some species. Turtles get caught in the plastic while trying to feed. And sometimes they eat nothing but plastic bags and starve to death. Every year plastic kills millions of birds, fish, turtles, seals and even dolphins."

"I had no idea," I said.

"Plastic is not fantastic, at least not in the ocean. And the sea, contrary to human thinking, is no garbage dump!"

"I never thought it was," said Maria.

"Me neither," I said.

Because we were on the other side of the earth, it was still night and the sun had not yet risen. But looking toward the east, I could see the sky turning a dull orange. Sunrise (our second of the day) was just minutes away.

"Do you hear that?" I asked.

"Hear what?" said Maria.

"Not sure," I said. "It sounds like surf."

"Is surf," said Delphis. "We're near the Pearl and Hermes Atoll, in the Northwestern Hawaiian Islands.

"What's an atoll (ăh-tall)?" Maria wanted to know.

"An atoll is a kind of coral island," I said, trying to remember the exact definition of atolls.

66

"Close," said Delphis. "Atolls are ring-shaped coral reefs. They are mostly underwater but they sometimes include small low-lying islands."

By now we could make out a line of surf shining in the moonlight. Beyond the surf stretched a small, treeless island, barely higher than the waves breaking on its beach.

"Atolls grace the wide neck of the Pacific like a chain of polished pearls," said Delphis. "Oh, that's so poetic, yes? But many atolls are so low they will disappear under the rising sea."

"Do people live on atolls?" I asked.

"Do," said Delphis. "One day they will have to leave their islands or else."

"Or else what?"

"Drown," said Delphis.

"Oh," said Maria.

Delphis glanced at the rising sun. "Time to go. One more stop and it's back to home waters."

Atolls are ring-shaped coral reefs. Many are in danger of being overtaken by sea level rise.

That was when we heard the scream.

We had just passed an "island" of wooden piers, furniture and other flotsam scattered around a half-submerged rooftop. From the rubbish came the screams of someone in distress.

The cries grew increasingly frantic as we got closer. I jumped onto a plank. That turned out to be a mistake. My feet went right into the water. With difficulty I scrambled onto more solid footing. Checking for nails, I made my way along a wide wooden beam slanting toward the roof.

"Anybody home?" I called out. The screams were desperate now. There came a mad scrambling from somewhere under the debris. Two pointed ears and a furry head emerged from a hole in the roof.

"Hello. What are you doing here?"

"Meow!"

I pulled the cat, a big gray and white tom with a long striped tail and green eyes, through the hole. Doubtless once well fed and sleek, it was now little more than skin and bones.

"It's a cat!" I called back to the others.

The cat jumped up on my shoulders and purred loudly, as I carefully retraced my steps.

"Poor cat," said Maria. "He must be thirsty. Give him some water from your water bottle, Arion."

I poured water onto my cupped hand. The cat lapped it up and meowed for more. I gave it the rest of our water.

"How can a cat survive a tsunami and who knows how many days at sea?" Maria asked.

"Nine lives," I said.

"The power of nature," said Delphis.

"Our third good deed for the day," Maria proudly proclaimed.

"We should start a sea critter rescue business," I suggested.

"Can we keep the cat, Delphis?" pleaded Maria. "At least until we can put it on shore?"

"Long as our saline feline friend doesn't object."

"We have to give him a name," insisted Maria.

But I already knew what the cat's name would be.

"Tsunami," I said. "His name is Tsunami."

Maria laughed. "What an intrepid band of travelers! Two humans, a magic dolphin and a hitchhiking cat named Tsunami!"

"Meow," agreed Tsunami.

Delphis laughed his peculiar dolphin laugh. "Move your dorsals, little friends. Time to go."

And off we went.

The world's oceans are filling up with trash. Plastic trash is especially harmful because it kills birds, turtles and other sea life.

8 The Island of the Blue Butterflies

The island was like nothing we'd seen before. Beyond the bright sandy beach lay a dense tropical rainforest, unbroken except for a space cleared at one end for a fishing village. From the jungle came the cries of insects and birds. And above the trees far to the east stood a range of tall mountains.

Delphis told us the island was one of many barrier islands lining the Pacific coast of Colombia. Its single village consisted of perhaps a dozen wooden shacks on stilts and some dugout canoes with outboard motors that had been dragged up on the beach. Next to the canoes stood a shack where a group of men were doing some kind of construction work.

"Why are they building a house so close to the water?" asked Maria.

"Not building," said Delphis. "They're unbuilding."

"They're doing what?" I said.

"Unbuilding. Taking the house apart and moving it back away from the water," he explained.

We watched the men take a wall down and drag it across the sand to the edge of the forest. Returning to the shack, they started taking apart the roof. In a few minutes they had stripped down the roof and part of another wall.

Delphis described what was happening. "As sea level rises, the fisher folk move the village back from the sea, house by house. Their homes are simple structures that can easily be taken apart and reassembled."

"Ah," said Maria. "This is the place you mentioned earlier, where people move their houses back with the retreating shoreline."

"This is the place," said Delphis.

"But why don't they just put their houses in the forest far from the beach?" I asked.

"Mosquitoes," he explained. "The jungle's full of 'em. Near the water the sea breeze keeps them away. No surprise then that the villagers choose to live on the beach, where the breeze is strong."

"It's the same where we live," noted Maria. "The mosquitoes are so bad in the summer everybody bolts to the beach."

"And don't forget the no-see-ums," I reminded her.

No-see-ums are a particularly nasty sand fly. They bite like an alligator and fly in clouds around your arms and legs and head, sometimes getting into your eyes and mouth and even up your nostrils. They're called no-see-ums because they're small and hard to see. About the only defense against a no-see-um attack is to dress up like an astronaut, cover your body with bug spray and hope for a strong wind.

"Mosquitoes are more than just a nuisance," said Delphis. "In the tropics they cause diseases like malaria. The humans here have no choice but to live on the beach."

"And that," said Delphis, with a click and a whistle, "is a problem when the island you live on is sinking."

"Sinking?" Maria said.

"Sinking."

"Why sinking?" I wanted to know.

"Earthquakes are frequent along these shores," Delphis explained. "When the earth shakes, the coastline sinks. Sometimes as much as 3 feet (1 m) in a day."

"I see the problem," said Maria. "Sea level rise is super fast here because the land is sinking."

"And because the icecaps are melting," I added. "Don't forget global warming."

"A double punch for Colombia," said Delphis. "Sea level rises so quickly here the fisher folk have to move their houses every 10 years or so."

By this time the men had moved most of the house back to the edge of the trees and were taking down the last remaining wall.

"Delphis," I said, trying to keep the worry out of my voice. "If there are earthquakes here, does that mean ... they have tsunamis?"

"Sometimes. But I don't think we'll get one today."

I relaxed. A little.

"Speaking of tsunamis," said Delphis. "How's our little furry friend?"

"As intrepid a traveller as any," I answered, trying to sound clever, even though I wasn't sure what "intrepid" meant and was too proud to ask my sister for a definition.

"He must be hungry," said Maria. "Can you get him some fish, Delphis?"

"Can. But first will have to put everyone on the beach."

"Fine by me," I said, thinking it'd be good to stretch my legs awhile.

Delphis took us along the shoreline away from the village. There was a stiff breeze coming from the ocean, but the surf was small and we fairly whizzed over the sea.

I looked across the ocean toward the west where the water sparkled like quartz crystals in the sunlight. A speedboat with twin outboards bounced toward the horizon, leaving a wake that resembled a pair of coiling sea serpents.

Somewhere beyond that blue horizon the discards of civilization swirled in a monstrous patch of garbage. And to the west, along the coast of Namibia, hungry lions feasted on what the waves washed ashore. And further still stretched the beaches of Morocco, where men stole sand to make concrete. And beyond Morocco, rose the seawalls and castles of England, defenders against maritime invasions. And far to the north, unseen by human eye, the Greenland ice sheet cracked and melted and dropped into the ocean. And the seas rose everywhere, filling up the ocean basins like a leaky faucet filling a plugged sink.

The world is so big, I thought. *Yet everything is connected. Plastic bags from a California beach kill sea turtles in the middle of the ocean. Ice melts in Greenland and sea level rises in Colombia.*

About a mile from the village Delphis slid up to the beach. Tsunami immediately jumped onto the sand. Seconds later Maria and I did the same.

"Be back soon," said Delphis, "with tasty fish for our intrepid friend."

At that moment a shout issued from the forest.

"Mira! Delphis!"

A boy and a girl emerged from the trees and came running across the beach toward us. The girl, who was about Maria's

73

age, stopped a few feet from the water. She had long, black hair and dark eyes with long lashes. She carried a leather pouch that clinked as she ran.

The boy was about my age or maybe a bit younger. He ran straight into the water, heedless of shoes and clothes, and threw his arms around Delphis.

There followed a long conversation in Spanish, of which I could understand nothing. The boy kept repeating the word "magico".

Finally, Delphis introduced everyone in a jumbled mix of English, Spanish and Dolphinese. The boy's name was Rio. His sister was Tierra. They lived in the village where their father worked as a fisherman. He was one of the men we saw moving the house back from the water.

"Do you know these kids?" I asked Delphis.

"Friends," he said.

Tierra spoke to Maria and pointed toward the jungle.

"She wants to show you something special in the trees," said Delphis.

"What about mosquitoes?" asked Maria.

"No worries," said Delphis. "Today's sea breeze is strong enough to keep mosquitoes away."

Tierra smiled shyly and gestured for us to follow.

"Back in a few minutes," said Delphis.

We marched single file across the beach into the jungle, Tierra leading, then Maria. Rio, tracking wet footprints and making squishy sounds, followed me. And last came Tsunami with his tail straight up, purring loudly, no doubt grateful to be on dry land again.

Tierra's pouch jingled as she walked. *Probably full of shells,* I guessed.

Entering the forest was like walking into a cool, dark room. As my eyes adjusted to the gloom, I could see we were following a narrow path bordered by thick trees. Shafts of sunlight penetrated the canopy like spotlights in a dark theater.

Nobody spoke. The sound of waves, our constant companion for the past several hours, faded and was replaced by the swish of wind gusting through the treetops. *I wonder if there are any poisonous snakes in the jungles here. If there are, we'll never see them in this dark forest.*

There was movement in the shadows on either side of the path. I caught glimpses of something blue flashing among the trees. But every time I turned to look, there was nothing there. Whatever it was, it seemed to be pacing us or at least going in the same direction.

Forest phantoms, I thought.

Tierra stopped and turned around. She whispered in Spanish and raised an index finger to her lips.

"Shhh," she said quietly.

Something rubbed against my ankle. I jumped. But it was just Tsunami.

"Shhh," I said.

We walked a little further into a small clearing in the forest. Tierra stepped to one side and pointed to a tree in the center of the clearing, its trunk covered with the biggest butterflies I'd ever seen. There must have been hundreds of giant blue butterflies gathered on that tree. Hundreds more, perhaps thousands, fluttered around the clearing like winged sapphires.

One perched on Maria's shoulder. I reached out. Touched its wings. The butterfly was bigger than my outstretched hand. It hopped onto my index finger, folded and unfolded its wings and then flew to the tree, where it merged into the pulsating blue mass.

Rio approached and pointed to the tree.

"Morpho azules," he said.

"Oh, blue morpho butterflies!" said Maria. "I remember reading about them. They are some of the biggest butterflies in the world."

"Must be a butterfly convention," I joked.

And then Tsunami went crazy.

One moment the cat was sitting calmly on the forest floor, licking a paw, occasionally glancing up when a morpho fluttered by. The next moment he was on his feet, fur raised, head turning from side to side as if straining to hear something. He was hissing fiercely.

Something is coming. Something big ... and bad.

A deep, resonant rumble like a fast-moving transfer truck boomed in our ears. The ground shook. A thousand butterflies took off in wild flight, transforming the clearing into a glowing blue cloud. Butterflies flew everywhere, brushing against our arms and faces, nearly blinding us. Tsunami ran straight up the tree.

As quickly as it had started, the shaking stopped. Maria and I looked at each other, wide-eyed and open-mouthed.

"Earthquake," she said.

"Terremoto," said Rio, laughing nervously.

We get earthquakes in Charleston sometimes. They are generally minor tremors, and like the one we just felt, pass quickly and are quickly forgotten. But earthquakes are always unnerving, even the small ones. Unlike a storm, there's no way to predict when one will hit. They knock on your front door like an unwelcome guest, when least expected and least wanted.

"We should go," Maria said.

"I think you're right," I agreed.

But Tsunami was still in the tree and no amount of coaxing would persuade him to come down. I started to climb.

Rio touched me on the shoulder. Before I could say anything, he shinnied up the tree as fast as any squirrel.

In our neighborhood I am recognized as the unofficial tree-climbing champion of the Carolinas. But that boy put me to shame. In a few heartbeats, he scrambled to the top of the tree, cradled Tsunami under his arm and then slid gracefully back to the ground.

"Awesome!" I said. "Thanks."

"De nada," he said.

Tsunami rubbed against Rio's legs and then high-tailed it back to the beach. I guess he'd had enough excitement for one day.

Delphis was waiting for us at the water's edge with several small fish. He tossed the fish onto the sand. Tsunami wasted no time. Taking a fish in his mouth, he sprinted a few paces down the beach. Growling fiercely, lest anyone steal his break-fast, he swallowed everything, including the head, in one gulp. Then he returned and grabbed another fish. And then another.

"Don't eat too fast," I warned. "You'll get sick."

With Delphis acting as interpreter, we said our goodbyes to our new friends.

"Thanks for rescuing Tsunami," I said to Rio.

"My pleasure," he answered.

"And thanks for showing us the butterflies," said Maria to Tierra. "That was fantastic."

Reaching into her pouch, Tierra pulled out a shell.

"This is for you," she said. "Something to remind you of our island."

She gave Maria a shell with polished bands of brown and white and blue stripes. It was beautiful. We found out later it was a Pacific Crown Conch, a kind of snail found on the Pacific coast from Mexico to Peru.

Maria put the shell to her ear. "I can hear the sea," she said. "The sea that's around your island."

Pacific Crown Conch

Maria gave Tierra the Scotch bonnet she'd found earlier that morning. "This is for you," she said, "so you can hear the sea from our island."

Tierra put the shell to her ear and smiled.

Delphis looked up at the sun, which I interpreted as the dolphin equivalent of a human looking at a watch, a not-so-subtle hint that it's time to go.

We waved goodbye as Delphis carried us out to sea. Tsunami, belly full and fully hydrated, sat purring on my lap. The last thing I saw before entering the fog were Rio and Tierra waving farewell from the distant beach.

And then off we went.

One way coastal towns can deal with sea level rise is to move back as the shoreline retreats.

e were cruising on a shallow sea toward an undiscovered horizon, passing in and out of shadows cast by by stray clouds. The sun was a golden flame high in the sky. Tsunami lay asleep on my lap, indifferent to the scenic beauty of the moment.

I didn't know cats could snore so loud.

The water was so clear we could see crabs and starfish and spiny lobsters with absurdly long antennae, creeping across the sandy bottom. Yellow and black striped fish darted between mountains of rainbow-hued coral just below the sea's surface. Giant groupers hovered ominously around the coral like Jurassic beasts. And once we cruised over the long, shadowy form of a shark. It might have been a black-tipped reef shark, but I couldn't be sure. We were moving too fast.

We passed a long stretch of reef which, for some reason, was a faded, dull gray color. The corals were still there, but they were missing their beautiful colors and their fish.

"What happened to the reef?" I asked.

"Dead," said Delphis, slowing down and circling back to where the reef was fish-filled and full of color.

"Why dead?" I asked.

"Global warming," he said. "A warmer atmosphere makes a warmer ocean. And a warmer ocean kills coral."

"Because of too much CO_2 (carbon dioxide) in the air?" I asked.

"Yep," said Delphis.

We were poised over the boundary between the still living reef and the dead zone, where patches of bleached coral stood like underwater tombstones, sad memorials to the foolishness of humanity.

"Coral reefs are dying around the world," said Delphis, speaking slowly to add gravity to his words. "This is unfortunate because reefs are home to 25% of all sea life."

That was when I saw the fin. It was about 100 feet (30 m) behind us, cutting through the water like a butcher knife, coming straight for us. And fast.

I read somewhere there are more than 400 species of sharks in the world. Some are as small as your hand. Others are longer than a car. This one was as big as a truck.

"Sh-sha ... " I couldn't get the word out. Not that it would have mattered. Delphis was lecturing about the perils of global warming. He and Maria were unaware of the looming danger.

Oh, this is not good, I thought. *Not good.*

The shark kept coming. It was so close now I could see its body. A single eye, pitiless and black as midnight, stared straight at me. Any second now the shark would attack.

And then a miracle happened. The animal swerved, traced a long, graceful half-circle in the water and continued on its previous path. Only now it was swimming away.

"Shark!" shouted Maria, pointing to the receding fin.

You think? My heart was pounding like a freight train.

"Sharks and dolphins are sworn enemies," said Delphis. "Still, you gotta respect an animal that's been around for more than 400 million years."

"That means they outlived the dinosaurs," I pointed out.

"Did," said Delphis. "But now they are disappearing from the world's oceans."

"How come?" asked Maria.

"Humans," said Delphis. "Humans eating too many fishes, including sharks. They survived the asteroid that wiped out the dinosaurs. The survived the ice ages. But they may not survive the Age of Man."

Delphis took us back across the reef, picking up speed until we were bouncing over the waves like a jet ski. Soon we entered deep water and the sea turned from turquoise to a dark blue-green.

I began to see sharks in a new light, as animals so tough, so rugged, so well adapted to their environment, they could survive anything, even an asteroid strike. They *did* command respect.

But now humans are wiping them out. *Does that seem right?*

Out of the corner of my eye, I caught sight of something breaking the surface. Without warning, a geyser of seawater exploded in front of us. Delphis abruptly swerved to avoid the spray, nearly tossing me off his back.

More columns of water hissed into the air. A tail the size of a garage door burst from the deep and slapped the surface, splattering us from head to foot with salt spray.

"Whales!" shouted Maria.

"No kidding," I said, wiping stinging saltwater from my eyes. Tsunami stretched and went back to sleep.

We had stumbled into a pod of sperm whales. I counted a dozen bodies sloshing the surface, including one giant, gaping mouth rising out of the water, as if trying to drink in the sky. Seawater mixed with globs of whale spit trickled down rows of teeth the color of day-old butter.

And then the Great Granddaddy of all whales, a true leviathan, leaped out of the sea directly into our path. Time slowed down as the whale rose ever higher, towering over us like a monstrous mountain of wet blubber.

Expecting Delphis to veer to one side or the other, I braced myself. But instead, with a powerful slapping of his tail, he took us right over the head of the whale, so close we could count the barnacles on its back.

I stared into an ancient, craggy and intelligent eye. The unblinking eye stared right back at me as the animal slipped into the sea. Gathering speed, the whale fell on its back with a boom that blasted spray high into the air. It reminded me of the calving ice we'd seen in Greenland.

I figured Delphis would glide back to the water as he'd always done before. But this time he took us higher and higher until the sea spread below us like a wrinkled, sun-washed blanket. Dwindling specks of white sparkled where whales were still playing. On the eastern horizon a stretch of pale green marked the outlines of the coral reef. A sailboat clawed its way across

the reef toward an island squatting in the hazy distance.

The sea is so big, I thought. *So full of life.*

By now we were level with the clouds, fluffs of white wonder that reminded me of kernels of giant popcorn. To my surprise we sailed straight into one of the clouds. Our world turned gray and for a long minute we saw nothing but a chilling mist. Icy beads of water condensed on our legs and arms. I shivered and not just from the chill. For some reason, being unable to see anything brought back my fear of heights.

If we fell from here it'd be like dropping onto concrete. We'd die for sure. I gripped Maria's waist more tightly, hoping she had a firm hold on Delphis's fin.

Finally we flew out of the cloud into the welcoming glow of the summer sun. Wind whistled through my hair. From some- where came the lonesome cry of gulls. The endless sea rolled from horizon to horizon, bounded only to the west by a flat, hazy coastline. So stunning was the view that I completely forgot my fear of heights.

"The earth is so beautiful," said Maria.

"What you call the earth we dolphins call … (a long whistle followed by several clicks). It loosely translates as 'Mother Ocean.' Remember our planet is mostly water and all life is birthed in the sea. Even your ancestors long ago crawled out of the deep."

The coastline became a stretch of sandy beaches lined with high-rise hotels, crowded streets and swimming pools. Beyond the beaches spread a wide bay, crossed by bridges and edged by a string of skyscrapers. So much water surrounded the city that the buildings seemed to grow like seaweed right out of the ocean.

A city on the sea, I thought. But there was something vaguely familiar about the place. I was sure I'd seen that city before, perhaps in a book or on television.

"Miami!" Maria said excitedly. "I recognize the skyline."

"Yep," whistled Delphis. "We're right off Miami Beach. One of the most developed barrier islands in the world."

As we began a slow descent toward the water, we passed a line of rocks curving seaward from a hotel.

"That looks like a groin," I said.

"Does," said Delphis. "Technically it's called a jetty. Same as

A jetty is like a groin, but is located at a harbor entrance or an inlet. Jetties keep sand from filling in a shipping channel.

a groin, but a jetty is a line of rocks along an entrance to a harbor or an inlet. Keeps sand from filling in the channel."

Delphis brought us gently down to the sea. We were perhaps a half-mile from the shore. I could just make out people fishing from the end of the jetty.

"Look closely," said Delphis. "See the sand piled up on one side of the jetty? A jetty traps sand (like a groin) which causes beach erosion somewhere else."

I remembered what Delphis taught us about longshore currents, how longshore currents move sand along a coast and how groins trap that sand, causing beaches further down the coast to erode.

"But you have to admit, the beach next to the jetty looks nice," commented Maria.

"It does," I agreed.

"Looks natural, too," said Delphis. "But it's not. The beach here is artificial."

"How can a beach be artificial?" asked Maria.

"Humans made it."

"People can make a beach?" I said. "That's weird."

"They use giant pumps known as dredges to pump sand from the sea floor onto the beach. They call it beach nourishment (also called beach replenishment). It's one way to slow down beach erosion."

"We should do the same for our island," I said, thinking out loud, "to keep our beach from eroding."

"That's it!" said Maria. "We could pump sand onto the beach. It would keep our house safe from storms."

"Would," said Delphis. "But pumping sand kills marine life on the ocean floor. Also kills all the critters living on the beach."

"I hadn't thought of that," said Maria.

"Expensive too. Costs millions."

I wondered how long it would take to raise a million dollars. *With my current allowance of ten dollars a month times twelve months in a year, that's 120 dollars a year ... A million divided by a hundred and twenty equals how many years?*

I tried to work the math in my head. *Might take a while,* I concluded.

"And nourished beaches don't last long," said Delphis. "A big storm can remove all that new sand in one day. And then you have to spend more money pumping more sand onto the beach. And so on and so on."

"Remember the hard lesson Julius Caesar learned?" he continued.

"Nobody commands the sea," I said, recalling our visit to England.

From somewhere came the mournful cry of seabirds. The wind began to pick up. Delphis turned north and took us rapidly up the coast of Florida. We passed more high-rises, condos, apartments, office buildings, hotels and houses.

It's a wonder the entire state doesn't sink beneath the weight of all those buildings.

The day was warming up like a frying pan. Even with the breeze I was sweating. I felt a tickling sensation as a bead of sweat rolled down my forehead to the tip of my nose, where it hung for a moment and then dropped. I watched it disappear from sight, merging with the infinite waters around us.

"Once long ago," said Delphis, "the world was warmer and the icecaps had mostly melted. This land you call Florida was at the bottom of a shallow sea. Now the sea is coming again. Coming to retake the lands it once ruled."

"What's going to happen to Miami," asked Maria, "when the sea really starts to rise?"

"What indeed?" said Delphis. "In Colombia you saw persons moving a village, house by house, back from the sea. But how can you move a big city like Miami with its heavy towers of glass and steel?"

Delphis emphasized his point with a series of rapid clicks.

"Humans always want to live close to the water. And the closer the better, they think! But they do not consider the risks of coastal living in an age of rising seas."

"To put it another way," he said, "humans need to learn how to think like the sea."

"Think like the sea," I said. "I like that."

"Sea level rise is no great hardship for dolphins," he continued, laughing his dolphin laugh. "Just means more space, more room for swimming (and more delicious fishes!). But humans ... Humans are different. Your kind has no fins. How will you swim to safety when your cities are flooded? How will you escape the rising waters?"

Except for the whisper of wind and waves all was quiet. Peaceful. I thought about what Delphis was saying. I thought about the joys of living next to the beach. And then I thought about the stress and worry brought by storms, beach erosion and sea level rise. *Does it make sense to live near the sea when you know that one day the sea will take your house?*

Delphis interrupted my thoughts. "Ah, the sea," he said. "Lovely, beautiful, bountiful, miraculous, wondrous sea. The waters of life. Home sweet home."

He blew a long column of spray out his blowhole. The wind brought the spray back over us which, under the sweltering Florida sun, felt pleasantly cool.

"Well, friends. Been a marvelous journey, full of wonderments and adventures. But all good journeys must end. Time to bring young humans home."

And then off we went.

Pumping sand on beaches to fight erosion is called beach nourishment. It is only a temporary solution. It is also expensive and kills the animals living on the beach.

90

10 Lighthouse

hen the fog cleared we found ourselves on home waters. The old lighthouse stood solemnly a couple of miles to the south, its weathered red and white stripes just visible in the distance. Beyond the lighthouse stretched a thin green line that was our island. Our home.

We were cutting across the channel to Charleston Harbor. Two long jetties spread seaward from both sides of the channel like a pair of arms welcoming incoming ships. Sand had piled up on the north side of one of the jetties. Beyond the jetties lay a series of groins.

Then it hit me.

Groins and jetties, I thought. *Holy smokes! That's it!*

"That's it! I got it!" I cried out loud. "It's the jetty!"

Delphis slowed down. Turned his head to look at me.

"Problem, little friend?"

"I figured it out!" I said. "The Charleston jetty! That's why the old lighthouse is losing sand, why the beach is eroding." I was so excited I could hardly get the words out.

"It's the jetty!" I repeated. "Don't you see?"

"Of course!" said Maria. "The jetty is trapping sand carried by the longshore current, starving Morris Island of sand. That's why the shoreline is retreating. I don't know why we didn't think of it before."

Delphis let out a long dolphin laugh. He kept on laughing. Soon Maria and I started laughing. We were all laughing so hard our eyes became watery. I think if cats could laugh Tsunami would have joined us.

After a while our laughter abated. Delphis whistled and said, "Clever little friends! A credit to your species you are! Was hoping you would see the connection between local beach erosion and the jetties. That's why I brought you this way."

"Humans built the jetties in the late 1800s to keep the harbor channel from filling in with sand. Almost immediately the beach at the old lighthouse began eroding."

"And now the lighthouse is in the sea," said Maria.

"That reminds me," said Delphis. "Do you know why fish are so smart?"

"I give up," I said. "Why?"

"Because they're always in schools!"

"Good one," said Maria.

"Humor," said Delphis. "Never leave home without it."

"You might say," I added, "humor is the main 'porpoise' to life."

"Very punny," said Maria.

We were drawing close to the Morris Island Lighthouse, so faded and weather-beaten that it seemed as much a part of nature as any rock or dune. It was low tide and the lighthouse stood high and dry on the sand, looking as if it had been standing there a thousand years and would stand for another thousand.

But I knew better. In a year or ten years or a hundred years the sea would knock it down and pound its bricks into rounded rubble and the lighthouse would stand no more. Like Sandown Castle in England, the sea would grind the old lighthouse into a pile of broken memories. Undersea archaeologists might comb its ruins for artifacts perhaps, but for the rest of the world the lighthouse would endure only as a paragraph in the history books. Nothing more.

Delphis took us in a wide arc seaward of the lighthouse, where it was deep enough for safe passage. And then just like that, we were back to our little island home, arriving at the very place where we'd found the Magic Dolphin, wrapped up in a fishnet. We could see the net where the tide had left it, now some distance from the water's edge.

Maria and I hopped awkwardly onto dry land, our legs stiff from sitting for so long. Tsunami jumped onto the beach. He approached the net. Sniffed suspiciously. Assured the object presented no danger, he started cleaning a paw.

"The journey ends where it began," said Delphis. "It's been a whale of a trip. You've seen more beaches in one morning than most persons see in a lifetime. Tell me what you learned."

We stood quietly for a moment, reflecting on all that we had seen and done since last night's storm.

"Not sure where to begin," said Maria. "I guess the first thing we learned is that beaches are moving."

"They're retreating," I said, "because of sea level rise."

"And sea level is rising because the glaciers are melting and the warming sea is expanding," added Maria.

"Like bicycle tires on a hot day."

I remembered our visit to Deal. "We learned that seawalls destroy beaches."

"And groins and jetties also destroy beaches. They trap sand that normally moves with the longshore current."

"Don't forget beach mining," I said.

"That's right. People mine beaches to get sand, but mining a beach is a form of erosion."

"That hurts the critters living on the beach," I added.

"We learned that beach erosion is a problem for people living near a beach," Maria said.

"But the beach life will retreat with the shoreline," I said.

"At least on a natural beach like the one in Namibia."

"We found out," I said, with a shudder, "that some beaches have lions on them."

"We saw how plastic is a big problem for the ocean. It kills turtles and other sea life."

"And we learned what can happen to folks living on a coast where tsunamis occur. Isn't that right, Tsunami?"

Tsunami, still busy cleaning himself, ignored my question.

"We discovered that coral reefs are dying," said Maria.

"You taught us about beach nourishment. It's expensive and kills the beach life," I recalled.

94

"And it doesn't work, at least not for very long."

"We learned," I concluded, "to think like the sea."

"Outstanding!" said Delphis.

Then after his customary mix of clicks and whistles and other dolphin chatter, he continued, "But what about your home? Are you any closer to keeping your home away from the jaws of the ever-hungry sea?"

I glanced at my sister. She pretended to study her feet. No one spoke for a long minute.

I looked out at the beautiful, mysterious, world-encircling sea. Mother Ocean, the cradle of our species, the source of our food and water and (as I later learned) most of our oxygen.

For me, Miami had been the clincher. Seeing all those high-rise buildings right on the beach and knowing there was no way they could be moved. Knowing, as Delphis had put it, that the sea was coming to "retake the lands it had once ruled." After seeing Miami Beach, I knew what we had to do.

"Retreat," I said, simply. "We have to move back from the sea."

Maria sighed. "I agree," she said. "And the sooner, the better. Before the next storm comes."

"Very wise," said Delphis, with a barrage of clicks and whistles. "You see what your elders see not."

And then Maria asked a question. The same question that had been crouching in the shadows of my thoughts from the moment we had met Delphis.

"Who are you, Delphis? I mean, who are you really? Dolphins don't just wash up on a beach and then start talking."

"And they sure as heck don't fly kids around the world," I added.

"Nor do they have scientific training."

"And they don't tell jokes."

Delphis "laughed" and directed a column of spray high into the sky like a sprinkler. The wind carried the spray out to sea. He blew spray again, forming a ring, like a smoke ring. The ring hovered a moment and then dispersed seaward.

"Let's just say I've been given certain powers. Powers I use to teach young humans how to live with the sea."

"Is that why Rio and Tierra knew you?" asked Maria. "But why teach kids? Why not talk to the president or somebody important?"

"The elders of your kind are slow learners. Their minds are as hard as coral. Young minds are quick as the wind and supple as seawater. Young minds learn fast. Learn best."

"Consider the lighthouse," he continued. "Built to warn mariners of a dangerous shoreline. You must be a lighthouse for your species. With the light of your new knowledge, flash a warning so others may know of the coming of the sea. Light the way so all will live in harmony with the sea."

"Is that the favor you wanted us to do?" asked Maria. "To tell other people about how to live with the sea?"

"Yes," he said.

"We'll do it," I said.

And then Delphis spoke for the last time. "The hour is late. Time to say farewell."

"Will we see you again?" asked Maria.

"Will," he said. "If not in this world, then in dreams."

Maria gave Delphis a long hug. "Thank you for being such a good teacher."

I couldn't think of anything to say, so I just waded into the water, unmindful of my "new" sneakers and touched the top of his head.

That was the last we saw of the Magic Dolphin. As we watched, he began to glow ever so faintly like a candle. His body slowly became transparent. Starting with his tail and continuing toward his head, he began to shimmer and ripple like water. The ripples got larger until he disappeared entirely.

For a long while a dolphin smile remained, until that too faded and became one with the sea.

Be a lighthouse. Shine the light of your knowledge on the world so others may learn to live in harmony with the sea.

11 Dream of the Sea

rom far away the laughter of gulls drifted across the water. Wind tickled my hair. The sun was a hot blanket smothering my upturned face. Flies buzzed my head. I must have dozed off. When I opened my eyes, Maria was standing a few feet away, studying the lighthouse. She was rubbing her eyes.

"I just had the strangest dream," she said. "It was about a magic dolphin."

"No way!" I stared at her open-mouthed. "I had the same dream!"

"Then it was only a dream? Delphis? Greenland? All ... just a dream?"

Of course, I thought. *It couldn't have been real. Kids don't fly around the world on the backs of dolphins!*

Maria recounted the details of her dream.

"Strange that we had the same dream," I said.

"Maybe it was telepathy," she said.

"But it seemed so real!" I protested.

I examined the old lighthouse, leaning ever so slightly seaward. *At least the lighthouse is real.*

"We'd better get back home soon," said Maria. "Mom and Dad will be worried. It's already way past lunchtime."

"Yeah," I said, looking at the sun. "I think you're right."

At that moment there came a rustling from where the forest topped the dunes. A large, gray and white striped tomcat came bounding across the sand toward us.

"Tsunami!" I cried.

The cat rubbed against my sneakers — my white sneakers, which every day for the past year had been an unmistakable bright shade of red.

Maria pulled something out of her pocket and held it up for me to see. It was a small shell with purple and white stripes, a shell not native to the Carolinas. The kind of shell you might find on an island off the west coast of South America.

Quickly I emptied the contents of my pack onto the beach. Out rolled several plastic bags, one empty water bottle, a sandy pocketknife, a half-eaten sandwich and one fist-sized specimen of chalk as white as any cliff in Dover.

"Wow," I said, shaking my head. "That is totally weird!"

I repacked my bag. Picking up the shells we'd collected

earlier that day, we turned toward home, Tsunami close behind.

On the way back I found six shark's teeth.

Maria and I never told anyone about the Magic Dolphin (not that people would have believed us). In the years that followed, we debated whether Delphis had been real or not. One or the other of us would explain our mutually shared adventures as hallucinations or a dream or as some other natural phenomenon grounded in hard science. Then we'd switch sides. One or the other would argue that there really had been a magic dolphin. Certainly the knowledge we'd gained was real enough. On that point we both agreed.

My pet theory was that Delphis had been a U.S. Navy experiment, a kind of genetically engineered super-dolphin who escaped his trainers and traveled the seven seas teaching kids about ocean ecology. But I knew that was unlikely. The technology to create such a being didn't exist. Not yet, at least.

After a while we gave up the debate and accepted that something inexplicable had happened. It was a mystery and some things in life will always be so. Maybe it's better that way.

It took a while, but eventually we convinced our parents to move away from the beach. We found a beautiful house sheltered in the forest a few miles from the ocean. Tsunami liked the place because of its squirrel-chasing opportunities. We were happy because the house was close enough to the sea that we could pedal our bikes there on the weekends. So we still collected shells, swam and otherwise enjoyed the beach, though of course, not as often as before. Except for the squirrels, everyone was happy.

Two years later, Hurricane Hendron, a Category 5 hurricane, blew up from the Caribbean and flattened the Charleston area with the ferocity of a giant bulldozer. It was a terrible disaster for all who lived on the coast. Our new home, on high ground and protected by trees, suffered minimal damage. But our old house got washed away in the storm surge. In fact, nearly every house on the island was smashed into toothpicks or was so badly damaged that the owners never came back.

Worse still, the old lighthouse got knocked down. What had once been a historic landmark is now a pile of broken bricks and twisted steel barely visible above the water at high tide.

The hurricane inspired Maria to become an architect. Her specialty is beach houses that fit in with nature and are stout enough to withstand most storms. Always insisting on keeping the dunes and trees in place for protection against hurricanes, she reminds her clients that one day they will have to leave their homes and retreat with the rising sea.

I became a coastal geologist. I write books about beach processes and teach classes at the university. Once a year I take my students on a field trip to the ruins of the old lighthouse. It's as good a place as any to talk about the risks of living on the coast.

Last summer Maria and I took our kids to the beach. We watched her daughter and my son build a sand castle at the edge of the surf. Unfortunately for them, the tide was rapidly coming in. As fast as the kids shoveled sand into a protective wall, the waves surged over and around the wall.

"A sand castle," Maria said. "The perfect metaphor for coastal living."

"Nobody stops the sea," I mused.

"Nope. Not even Caesar."

Suddenly the kids halted their labors, stood up and looked intently seaward.

"Look, Momma! Dolphins!"

"Three of 'em!"

We shaded our eyes and watched the dolphins slip through the water in perfect unison and with consummate grace.

"Did I tell you I'm writing a children's book about a magic dolphin?"

"Do you think it really happened ... you know, Delphis and all?" Maria spoke quietly, her eyes still following the dolphins.

"It was a dream," I said. "The dream of the sea."

"Think?"

We watched the dolphins grow steadily smaller as they moved down the coast, until finally fading from view.

"Actually, I don't think about it much anymore. Real or not, it was ... " I paused, searching for the right word.

"Magic," I said.

he first time was a complete surprise. He was swimming in the middle of his tank, thinking about snacking on more fish. All of a sudden he found himself on the far side of the tank next to the fish he'd just been thinking about. *What just happened?*

At first he thought he might be going crazy. Or that he had swum across the tank and had forgotten about it. *My memory must be failing,* he decided. But it happened again the next day. He was thinking about the other side of the tank, when suddenly he found himself on the opposite wall. With a shock, he realized that by picturing a location in his mind he could instantaneously transport himself to that location.

Imagination, he thought, *can be a most powerful tool.*

It took several "jumps" to polish his technique. The first few times made him feel sick, like his stomach had been turned inside out. But by the 10th or 11th time, the nausea was mostly gone and jumping from place to place had become as easy and as natural as swimming.

His newfound skill was great fun. Sometimes during a lesson he would play tricks on his trainers. He'd vanish and reappear behind them without warning. Or he'd reappear in the deepest part of the tank where nobody could see him. Once he even levitated in the air near the ceiling, directly above his trainers. They never saw him and they never figured out what was going on.

Eventually, the inevitable happened. The world became "fuzzy" like a fog. The walls and floors of his tank disappeared and water stretched in all directions. Fish of all kinds swam everywhere. And shining overhead where the ceiling used to be was something he'd never before seen in real life — the bright golden orb of the sun. With a wild surmise he realized he had jumped to the sea!

I should return to my tank. But no ... think I'll explore this new world a bit first.

Time passed. The years piled up like sediments on the seafloor. He journeyed everywhere, from the cold waters of the poles to the warm tropics, from sea to sea, from shore to shore. Sometimes he joined pods of other dolphins, learned their customs, their language. But he never really felt at home with them and they never really accepted him as one of their own. *Genetically enhanced intelligence has its disadvantages,* he thought. *It endows you with powers that seem like magic, but it also makes you feel separate from the world. Lonely.*

He began to yearn for the company of humans. He missed talking with his trainers. He especially missed learning new jokes. At the same time, he saw how humans were making a mess of the world's oceans. For one thing, they were eating too many fishes, leaving little for dolphins and other sea life. They were ruining beaches with seawalls and groins and by sand mining. And they were putting too much plastic, too many bad chemicals and other wastes into the water. They seemed to regard the ocean as a giant garbage dump and beaches as their personal playgrounds.

And then there was carbon dioxide. He didn't mind humans releasing so much CO_2, which trapped heat from the sun and caused glaciers to melt, which in turn triggered sea level rise.

The more water, the more fun, at least as far as a dolphin was concerned. But the real problem with CO_2 was that it seeped into the ocean and became carbonic acid. The acid (along with warmer seawater caused by a warmer atmosphere) was killing marine life, especially the coral reefs. Reefs he had visited years before that had been bright and colorful and full of fish and other life were now a dull bleached-white color, completely void of living things. *If humans don't stop producing CO_2 there won't be any more reefs left in the sea.*

He often wondered why humans couldn't see how their lives, how all life depends on the sea for its existence. *Don't they know most of their oxygen comes from the sea? Don't they understand that the sea is dying?*

Problems... problems. What to do?

And then the answer came. The little humans were the key, he realized. He must teach them to be good stewards of the sea. Teach them to love the sea, to take care of Mother Ocean, for she is sick and needs help.

But how to meet young humans? They never enter deep water. And he was no good on land. He couldn't just jump into a classroom and say, "Hi there. Today's lesson will be about sea level rise." This was a real puzzler. A true conundrum. And it took the better part of a year before he finally resolved the issue.

What was needed, Delphis decided, *was a really big storm and a fishnet ...*

The typhoon blew itself out overnight. Most of the houses were high on the slopes of the mountain and so were unaffected by the storm waves. Other than a few roof tiles knocked off by the wind and some trees blown over, the village was largely undamaged. As usual, the fishermen were up early preparing their boats for another busy day working the reefs.

One of the men stood on the dock with a sour look on his face, cursing under his breath. He was sure he had securely tied his net to his boat the day before. The boat was there. But the net was gone, nowhere to be found.

Must have blown away in the storm, he thought. *Bad luck.*

While his father searched in vain for his net, Kai and his friend Taka were on the beach looking for the shells they knew the storm had washed in. It was a good day for beachcombing. Except for a pair of sea hawks circling overhead, the beach was completely deserted. They walked the long stretch of sand from harbor to cliff face, picking up shells along the way. Kai even found an argonaut egg case, a rare and beautiful shell.

Argonaut egg case

"A gift from the sea," he called it.

When the boys could walk no further, they turned to head back. That was when Taka spotted the pile of driftwood.

"Might be some more shells over there," he said.

But as they approached the pile, they soon realized it wasn't driftwood at all. It was something else. And it was stirring.

"Look! A dolphin wrapped in a net!"

"Free me," said the dolphin.

The END

Author and Illustrator

Charles Pilkey is a former geologist turned freelance artist, writer and illustrator. His love affair with the sea began when he was a kid growing up on Sapelo Island, a wildly beautiful barrier island off the coast of Georgia. The inspiration for *The Magic Dolphin* came from a childhood memory of a day when he and his father found a pilot whale washed ashore on a Sapelo beach. With the help of friends, they set the animal free.

Although *The Magic Dolphin* is a work of fiction, the events described in the book are scientifically and/or historically accurate. Many are based on the personal experiences and observations of the author (cats able to sense an impending earthquake, the sounds of ice calving, sperm whales broaching off the Florida coast and so on). As to whether a genetically enhanced, talking dolphin will one day grace the world's oceans ... we shall see.

Visit Charles Pilkey at **technozoicdreams.com**

108

Consultant

Orrin Pilkey is the James B. Duke Professor Emeritus of Geology at the Nicholas School of the Environment at Duke University. He has visited beaches on all seven continents and has written a number of books about the future of beaches in an age of rising seas, including *The Rising Sea, The Last Beach, The Corps and*  *the Shore, Global Climate Change, and Retreat From the Rising Sea.* He also co-wrote with his son Charles, *Lessons From the Sand*, a beach science activity book for families visiting Carolina beaches.

Visit Orrin Pilkey at **nicholas.duke.edu**

84411057R00069

Made in the USA
Lexington, KY
22 March 2018